FOLLOW THE STONE

an Emmett Love Western - Volume 1

John Locke

This book is a work of fiction. Names, characters, places and incidents are either the product of the author's imagination or are used fictitiously. Any resemblance to actual persons, living or dead, or to actual events or locales is entirely coincidental.

FOLLOW THE STONE

Cover Designed by: Telemachus Press, LLC

Cover Art :
Copyright © istockphoto 2063584/Kamaga
Copyright © istockphoto 21929821/bubaone

Edited by: Winslow Eliot
http://www.winsloweliot.com

Published by: Telemachus Press, LLC
http://www.telemachuspress.com

Visit the author website: http://www.DonovanCreed.com

ISBN: 978-1-935670-47-6 (eBook)
ISBN: 978-1-935670-48-3 (Paperback)

Printed in the United States of America

10 9 8 7 6 5 4 3 2 1

FOLLOW THE STONE

"When the legend becomes fact, print the legend."

–The Man Who Shot Liberty Valance

CHAPTER 1

I HELD THE reins low while we walked, so Major could stretch his neck and toss his head if it pleased him. We'd done thirty miles over steep Ozark trails, and he was gettin' pissed. He'd earned his sorghum hours ago and knew it. But I was determined to camp on the banks of the Gasconade, and we were eight miles shy.

I rubbed Major's neck. "Soon," I said.

He blew a loud snort, which I won't bother translatin'.

It was late September, 1860, and we were north of Devils Rock, Missouri, where the air's cool to the nostril this time of year, and scented with honeysuckle. A stand of short leaf pine lined the right side of the trail and ran deep as the eye could see. Limestone cliffs and mud bluffs dotted with pink dogwood towered above us on the left. A soft breeze pushed us eastward, mile after weary mile.

It was nearin' dusk when I saw the five small stones on the path.

I pulled back on the reins and slid off Major's back and tied him to a pine bough. He took the opportunity to chew what grass he could pull from the pine needles.

Shrug had arranged the stones as he always did, North, South, East and West, with the fifth stone pointin' in the direction he was headin'. I was annoyed to see the fifth stone at the north-west point. Shrug knew I loved fishin' the Gasconade, and since he, too, had a passion for Nade perch, I was perplexed he would knowin'ly head the wrong way. But Shrug was the best scout in the territory, always had a reason for his actions, so I quietly cursed and climbed back on my horse and followed the stone.

Ten minutes into the ride we hit a clearin', where I found a circle of stones that ringed a single footprint, the cause of our detour.

It was a woman's shoe print.

I was so stunned I nearly fell off my horse.

I looked around. It was so crazy uncommon to find a woman's shoe print in this part of the wilderness, I wondered if perhaps Shrug had played a trick on me. I climbed off Major's back and knelt down beside the shoe print and studied it carefully while thinkin' *a talkin' horse, a tree that lays eggs, a flyin' pig–would make more sense.* And yet...

It was real.

I looked around again, this time for a stone that'd show me where he went. There was none. I'm no skilled tracker, but I managed to follow the lady's shoe prints to the edge of the forest. I had no idea how old the prints were, but I figured 'em fresh, or Shrug wouldn't a' changed course. Maybe he'd find her and bring her back alive. More likely, he'd find evidence she'd been carried off by a pack of wolves or a bear.

But Shrug didn't intend us to follow him into the forest, or he'd a' left a fifth stone.

Which he didn't.

"No fish for dinner," I hollered to Major. "Let's make camp."

I ain't ashamed to admit I talk to my horse more than I should. But we been together a long time, and Major's good company. I got a witchy friend, Rose, who travels with me from time to time. It's her opinion that Major can follow the spirit of my words, and I 'spect she's right.

I took a bowl from my kit and poured some water in it and let Major drink it dry. I was about to pour some more when, from deep in the woods, I heard a woman scream.

CHAPTER 2

THE FIRST SCREAM was followed by a second, then the screamin' stopped. I added water to Major's bowl, and watched him drink.

"Well, she just saw Shrug, or whatever it is he's savin' her from," I said. "Which means she's still alive. Or was, 'til that last scream."

When Major finished drinkin' his fill, I tied him to a saplin' and removed my kit, blankets, and saddle from his back. Then I gathered some rocks and arranged 'em to hold a coffee pot and fryin' pan, and put some wood between 'em, and enough kindlin' to get things goin'. The first match worked, so I filled the coffee pot with water from a canteen and put it on my rock stove. Then I pulled my rifle from the scabbard and headed out to see if I could scare up a rabbit or two.

I couldn't.

I only tried for twenty minutes, and wouldn't a' given up so soon had I not heard Major's whinny. I headed back to camp and was dumbfounded to see a tangle-haired woman spoonin' something I took to be coffee, into my pot. She hadn't seen or heard me yet.

I froze where I stood among the poplars, then ducked down and surveyed the scene.

She was alone, busyin' herself with the coffee. I wondered if she'd gone through my things to get it, then realized from the smell it was her coffee. Probably got it from the huge carpetbag sittin' on the ground, left of the fire. While I didn't sense danger, I also never had a lone woman walk into my camp before, so I whistled the song a wood warbler makes, and got a similar response from a half mile away. The response had come from Shrug, which meant everything was as okay as it was likely to get. I stood and made some noise as I walked into camp, so as not to spook her.

"Where's the food?" she said, lookin' up from the coffee pot.

I had to stop where I stood a minute, caught up in her eyes. They were cornflower blue, a color I'd never seen in a person's eyes before. She wiped her hands on her skirt, then tried to smooth her hair, gave up, and waited for me to respond.

I said, "Excuse me?"

"Wayne said you were bringing food."

"What? Who?"

"Are you daft? He didn't tell me you were daft."

Her eyes had me transfixed. It felt like she was borin' holes into my soul. She had the kind of eyes that could shame a man quickly, and get him to church when he'd rather be drinkin'. I forced my gaze lower. She had tiny, precise feet, somethin' I'd noticed from the tracks.

"Ma'am," I said, "If you're talkin' about Shrug, well, he don't speak."

"Shrug? Is that his surname?"

I wondered if I might be dealin' with a crazy woman. I guess she caught the look of concern in my mind, for she eyed me carefully, and crept slowly toward her carpetbag. Probably had a gun in there she couldn't shoot.

"Who are you, sir? Please, identify yourself at once."

"I'm Emmett Love."

She stopped tryin' to get to her bag and looked confused a moment, then said, "Are there more than two of you?"

"Two of me?"

She seemed exasperated, and began speakin' deliberately, as if to a child. "No, Emmett. Are there more than two of you men up here on the mountain?"

I removed my hat and ran my fingers through my hair while tryin' to cipher what she was askin'.

I said, "It's a big mountain, and I don't know how many men might be on it. But in this area, far as I know, it's just you and me and Shrug."

She frowned, and shook her head.

"You must have heard me scream," she said.

"Yes, ma'am, and a fine scream it was. By the second one, I had you pinpointed."

"You did."

"Yes, ma'am."

"And yet you moved not a muscle to come to my aid."

"No, ma'am."

"And why is that?"

"Well, if Shrug needed my help, he would a' whistled."

"Whistled."

"Yes, ma'am."

She gave me a look that might have had disgust in it. "So you're neither hunter nor hero. Are you a coward, then?"

I felt a burn creep up the back of my neck.

"A coward?" I scowled and put my hat back on, tired of her disrespect.

"That's right," she said. "After all, I need to know what type of person I'm dining with. Perhaps you're just lazy."

I'd never known a proper woman to have such a sharp tongue. I doubted she had a husband. If she did, he probably cut her loose. I shook my head and spoke in my strictest voice.

"I cut my huntin' short on account of my horse."

She looked at Major. "How so?"

"He announced you were enterin' camp."

"I see," she said with a smart tone. "Your horse talks, but your friend does not."

I sighed. This tenderfoot was lucky to be alive. I knew seasoned trappers who couldn't survive an Ozark night. Forgettin' that, her insultin' nature alone could get her killed by any number of men I know and admire. I worked to keep the anger outta my voice, but I'm sure some leaked out anyway.

"Ma'am, checkin' on my horse don't mean I can't hunt. And trustin' my friend's ability to handle trouble don't make me a coward, nor lazy."

We gave each other stern looks until I wondered if Shrug would care if I put a bullet through one of her hands, to soften her temperament. If I shot the fleshy web between her thumb and forefinger, she'd heal in a week or two. As a bonus, there'd always be a circle scar to keep her reminded.

Abruptly, she said, "Perhaps you're right. After all, I'm the outsider here. I shouldn't rush to judge. I've had a harrowing time, and I'm new to your ways. Forgive me, please." She approached me, extending her hand. "I'm Phoebe Thayer, of the Philadelphia Thayers."

I hesitated briefly, then wiped my hand on my shirt and took hers and shook it while thinkin' how close she'd come to losin' the use of it. But then, standin' a mere two feet from her, close enough to smell her scent, I began to think less about her hard words and more about her soft physical features.

She sensed the change in my mood, and pulled away, sayin', "I noticed your friend had neither horse nor gun."

"Shrug can't ride a horse, and don't need a gun."

"How can a man survive in the wilderness without a mount and gun?"

"Shrug ain't a normal man. On certain terrain he can move faster than a horse. On the plains, he's still plenty swift."

"Well, how does he protect himself?"

"He's an uncommon rock thrower."

"A rock thrower," she repeated.

"Yes, ma'am. He's got some sharp ones he throws vertical."

"I'm afraid I don't understand."

"I've seen Shrug slice a man's ears clean off with nothin' more than two sharp rocks flung from a short distance."

"That's preposterous!"

I removed my hat and gestured at the pot. "Is that sissy coffee any good?"

"I'm known for my coffee."

"You pourin'?"

She smiled. It was a small smile, but a pleasant one, just the same.

"You haven't asked how I came to be here or where I'm headed," she said.

"I tend not to ask people much, nor ask much of 'em."

I fetched my cup from my kit and let her pour some coffee into it. Up close I could see that her face, though smudged with grime, was smooth, and her features delicate and fine. Like all women, she had on twice the clothes she needed, and the parts of 'em I could see were covered in dirt and mud.

"How long were you in the cave?" I said.

She appraised me with what appeared to be a new respect. "Who said anything about being in a cave?"

I pointed. "Your clothes."

She looked down at her dress and frowned, as though this were the first she'd thought to look at it.

"I thought you didn't ask people much."

"I generally don't. But you seemed to leave the door open on it. I marvel you're alive."

"Why? Because I'm a woman?"

"Well, there's that."

"And what, you think all women are helpless?"

"Don't matter what I think, it's what them bear and wolves think. A woman's scent is one they're not apt to associate with danger. It's a scent they'll pick up on and follow."

She considered my words. "You put that very delicately, for a Western man."

I waited.

"I was in the cave for one night." she said. "And a terrible night it was. I heard wolves howling. And they were getting closer. Had Wayne not come to my rescue, I fear I would have perished."

I nodded. Then said, "Who's Wayne?"

Phoebe looked at me as though I were feeble-minded. About that time Shrug slipped into camp with three rabbits hangin' from his belt.

Phoebe's face lit up. She said, "Wayne! Thank the dear Lord you've come back, and with food, no less."

She looked at me and my rifle. "He killed three rabbits without a gun!"

Implyin' I hadn't killed any with one.

I said, "Your screamin' probably scared them his way."

Shrug smiled.

I looked at him. "Wayne?" I said.

Shrug shrugged.

CHAPTER 3

PHOEBE CHATTERED AT us while me and Shrug skinned the rabbits. More than once we exchanged glances about it, but I let her ramble on, hopin' she'd be talked out by dinner. While Shrug cut the meat, I got the fryin' pan on the fire and put some sowbelly in it 'til a fine layer of fat coated the bottom. Then Shrug placed the rabbit pieces in the pan, and I fussed with 'em some, enjoyin' the sizzlin' sounds and heavenly scent that only pan fried rabbit can produce. By the time I got the rabbit crisp on both sides, we'd forgotten all about the perch I originally planned to cook.

When the rabbit was right, we divvied it up and Shrug put his part in his pocket and scampered outta camp like he always did. I kept the rest in the fryin' pan, removed it from the fire, and placed it on the ground between Phoebe and me.

Phoebe seemed upset that Shrug had left without speakin'.

She looked at me. "Where's he going?"

"He's standin' guard."

"Where?"

I gestured broadly. "Everywhere."

"Well, where will he sleep?"

"Shrug don't sleep."

"Well, of course he sleeps! Everyone sleeps."

I stared at her face, tryin' to figure her out. Most people, when you answer their questions, don't contradict you afterward. Phoebe seemed not to need me participatin' in our conversations.

"He talks, too," she added.

"Uh huh."

She frowned. "You act as though you don't believe me."

I sighed, and pushed our rabbit around in the pan 'til the pieces were cool enough to handle. I tasted some.

"That's damn good rabbit!" I said, with great enthusiasm.

She launched her hand toward my face to give me a hard slap. But my reflexes are even sharper than her tongue, and I caught her wrist long before her hand made contact.

"Let go of me!" she cried.

I wasn't sure I should. But there was a mess of rabbit in the pan with my name on it.

"Fine," I said. "But don't try to hit me again."

"I can't abide cursing," she said.

"Well, you better learn to, 'less you're headin' back east."

She sat and pouted awhile, but then the smell of dinner got to her and she tried some.

"This` is outstanding!" she said brightly, despite her mood.

In my experience, fried rabbit will bring folks together, even enemies.

"You're coffee's good, too," I said.

We chewed our rabbit.

"How long have you and Wayne been traveling together?" Phoebe asked.

"Maybe two years."

"And in all that time you've never heard him speak?"

"Nope."

"That seems inconceivable." She said. Then softened her tone. "I can't imagine what you must think of me, coming in here, barking at you like an angry dog. I seem to have lost my manners."

"You been through a lot."

"Yes."

We ate in silence 'til we finished. Then we shared the rest of her coffee. By and by she said, "What's wrong with him?"

"Shrug? What do you mean?"

"He looks like a haystack made out of bones."

"He's more sideways than upright," I agreed.

"His body is all scrunched up like an elderly man with a severe hunchback," she said. "He seems unable to walk upright, though he moves faster and quieter than any human I've ever witnessed."

I nodded.

"But he moves more like a sand crab than a man," Phoebe said.

"That's a good way to describe it," I said. "And it's true that when scamperin', Shrug covers a lot of ground."

"Do other people call him Shrug?"

"Some. But he's got lots of names."

"Such as?"

"Well, to me he's Shrug, and you call him Wayne. And Indians around here call him *Weeshack.*"

"Weeshack?"

"Means Grasshopper."

"Well, that seems disrespectful."

"Oh no, ma'am. Shrug is highly respected by the Indians. They tend to keep a wide berth when he's in the area."

She nodded, thoughtfully.

"What happened to him?" she said. "Do you know?"

I sat quiet a minute. Then said, "A cowboy told me Shrug got flattened in a stampede as a child, and kept growin' sideways afterward."

"Did you ask him about it?"

"Nope."

"Why not?"

"If Shrug wanted me to know, he'd a'said somethin', or signed it out. But I believe it. If there's one thing that rattles Shrug to this day, it's a stampede."

"You've been in one?"

"About four months ago, along the Arkansas River."

"Buffalo?"

"Nope."

"Wild horses?"

"Nope."

"Well, what type of stampede was it?" she said.

"Snappin' turtles."

"What? There's no such thing as a turtle stampede!"

"Tell that to Wayne."

She shook her head. "Speaking of Wayne..."

"Yes?"

"How can you sit there and tell me you didn't know he could speak?"

"It never come up."

She showed a look of disbelief. "How is that possible?"

"Shrug keeps to himself. We been together two years, but I only see him a few minutes a week, at most."

The dyin' fire cast a glow on Phoebe's face, then a shadow.

She said, "If I live to be a thousand, I'll never understand pioneer men."

"Don't worry," I said. "You won't live that long. Not out west."

CHAPTER 4

"I INTENDED TO ride the trains from Philadelphia to Wichita," Phoebe said, next mornin', while washin' her face with canteen water.

"Only the train don't go beyond Rolla," I said.

"My parents were grievously misinformed at the train station in Philly. Is it true that Wichita is four hundred miles?"

"From Rolla? It's all of that."

Phoebe said, "I searched the entire city of Rolla to see if anyone was planning a trip."

"And naturally they weren't. So what, you planned to walk all the way to Wichita?"

"Of course not. I was told if I could get to Waynesville, I could catch a stagecoach to Springfield. And another from there to Wichita."

"No stage has ever stopped in Waynesville that I know of," I said. "And the one they did have in Springfield went broke last month."

She frowned.

I said, "What's in Wichita that's so important?"

"My husband."

I looked at her left hand.

"You ain't wearin' a ring," I said.

"It's an arranged marriage."

"You're a mail order bride?"

"That's a harsh way to put it," she said. "Mr. Pickett and I have corresponded for six months. We've exchanged photographs. He's a widower with a wonderful ranch, and a comfortable house."

"He sent you a photograph?"

"Yes, of course."

"How you know it's him in the picture?"

"He's been vouched for by no less than the Wichita Justice of the Peace."

I figured the Wichita Justice of the Peace could be bought for ten grains of gold, but I didn't tell her that. Hell, if she was bent on marryin' a stranger, whoever Mr. Pickett was, he'd probably do. If not, Phoebe wouldn't face any shortage of marriage proposals in Wichita. Men outnumber women twenty to one there, and though sharp-tongued, she was as comely as any I'd seen.

"You set out on foot for Waynesville by yourself?"

"The man at the train station told me it wasn't far."

"When we get to Rolla, I want you to point out the man who told you that."

"I'm not going back to Rolla," Phoebe said.

"The hell you ain't," I said, catching her wrist in mid-slap.

"Let go of me!"

"You're gonna have to stop tryin' to hit people."

"You're going to have to stop cursing."

I gave her a hard look, then shook my head. Lord, she was pretty. "Okay," I said.

"Okay?"

"Hit me."

"What?"

"Hit me five times now, and I'll owe you five curses."

"You can't pay for curses in advance."

"Ma'am, five curses could fly out of my mouth in the same sentence."

"Why, that's a terrible thing to have to admit!"

"Maybe," I said. "But that don't make it less true." Then I said, "Me and Shrug are headin' to Rolla this mornin', and ought to be there by noon. On Wednesday we're escortin' some women from Rolla to Dodge City, by way of Springfield. Sorry to say, we hadn't planned on stoppin' in Wichita this trip, but Newton's only twenty miles away.

"Wait–you're actually going through Newton? Mr. Pickett's ranch is just a few miles north of there."

"Well, that makes sense. Newton's hopin' for a rail spur, and land's a bargain there, compared to Wichita. Anyway, you're more than welcome to ride with us," I said. "For a fee."

"How much?"

I thought a minute. Helpless as she was, I would've taken her for free, just to keep some crook or scoundrel from takin' advantage of her. But it'd be improper to make that type of offer. Phoebe had no horse, and probably couldn't shoot a gun. Eighty was a fair price. But she might say no to that much money. And she was powerful pretty.

"Twenty dollars, gold," I said.

"Mr. Pickett will pay the fee."

"And if he don't?"

She fell silent. Probably worrying Mr. Pickett might not be all she hoped.

"Ma'am..."

"Please. Call me Phoebe."

"Phoebe, if he don't pay the fee, I won't worry about it. I'd be honored to take you to Newton to meet your mail-order husband. And if he ain't the man you want, I'll take you to Wichita."

"And if things don't work out for me there?"

"Well, me and Shrug'll be comin' back through Wichita two weeks later, and we'll take you to Rolla and get you on a train back to Philadelphia.

Phoebe's mouth curled into a warm smile. Her cornflower blue eyes sparkled and danced and the look she gave me was as welcome as a dry log on a winter fire. I bit the inside of my lip while thinkin' Mr. Pickett a lucky man.

"Mr. Love," she said.

"Call me Emmett."

"Emmett, I'm going to say yes to your generous offer."

I nodded. "Okay, then."

We gathered up our gear and I leaned over and interlocked my fingers to give her a leg up onto Major's back. She placed her tiny foot in my hands, and said, "Four hundred miles is a long journey."

"Yes ma'am, it is. And a dangerous one, too."

"It will probably be very difficult for you to refrain from using profanity," she said.

I chuckled. "S'pect you're right about that."

She hauled off and slapped the shit out of me, five times.

CHAPTER 5

WITH ITS TREE-LINED streets and mountain views, Rolla, Missouri, was one of the prettier towns I'd seen east of the Colorado territory. Compared to Newton, Kansas, where Phoebe was headed, it was like the Garden of Eden. When I walked into town leadin' Major behind me, Phoebe in the saddle, the first building we came upon that I hadn't seen before was the new court house.

"Well, I guess that ends the battle," I said.

"What battle?" Phoebe asked.

"They've been fightin' with Dillon to see which town would be named the County Seat. This new court house ought to wrap things up."

We stopped long enough for me to strap on my gun belt. Then we started movin' again, toward Miss Patty's Boardin' House.

"Where's Wayne?"

"Shrug don't enter towns much."

"Why not?"

"People laugh and point at him."

"That's abominable. He saved my life."

"He saved lots of lives, but folks don't know it to look at him."

We passed the train station.

Phoebe said, "How did such a small town manage to get train service?"

"A railroad contractor name of Bishop moved here. Had he moved to Cherryville, they'd a' got the rails. Rolla's little, but it's pretty, don't you think?"

"I haven't got eyes for it. My experience here was quite unpleasant."

"Well, maybe it'll grow on you this time."

"I doubt it."

"You know much about the place?"

"No. And don't care to."

"Rolla's only been a town for two years," I said. "It's named for Raleigh, North Carolina. Ever been there?"

"No."

"When the locals held a vote to name the town, a bunch from Raleigh said they could get families to move here if they named it Raleigh. They won the vote, but the folks here pronounced it Rolla, and that's how it's been ever since."

"I wonder why you think I care," she said.

"It'd be like if you move to Newton and everyone there calls you Feeba."

"That's absurd. I wouldn't stand for it."

"Not much you could do about it, I s'pect."

I tied Major to the rail in front of Miss Patty's, and Phoebe slid off the saddle.

"I'm glad you did that," I said.

"What, dismounted?"

"Yup."

"Why?"

"Well, to tell the truth, I wasn't quite sure how to help you down. I never seen anyone ride side saddle before. Makes for a comfortable ride, I s'pect, if a woman's bottom is narrow enough to fit."

"Mr. Love, I suggest you keep such thoughts about women's bottoms to yourself."

"Well, it's a compliment, really, to have such a nice one."

"Am I to expect similar comments from the men in Kansas? Or is just your mouth that's as foul as a soldier's latrine?"

I smiled. "I s'pect most Kansas men should know a fine rear end when they see one. Whether they'll comment on it as honestly as me is another issue."

"That's enough!" she said, though I could swear she seemed about to smile while sayin' it.

"Emmett?"

I turned to see Hollis Ford walkin' toward us, Hollis bein' Sheriff of Phelps County.

I said, "Hollis."

Hollis wore his gun belt low, his holster tied to his leg with a rawhide strap.

"You puttin' together another haul?" he said.

"I plan to."

"There's been a few askin' about you. Two or three at Shingle's, a few more at Lick and Casey's."

"I'll speak to 'em. Any mail orders?"

Hollis looked at Phoebe. "Looks like you found the one I know about. She goin' with you?"

"She is."

Hollis was quiet a moment. "I see you're heeled."

"Thought it wise."

"There's no trouble here that I know about."

"Glad to hear it."

Holllis went quiet again, content to stare at me. I stared back. Then he said, "When you plan to head out?"

Thing is, I don't like folks to know when I'm leavin' a place. As a known gun hand, I sometimes ruffle feathers in the towns I visit, and them that know when I'm leavin' might set out to bushwhack me.

"Wednesday, after breakfast," I said, knowin' it weren't true.

"Around nine?"

"Probably closer to ten."

"I'll spread the word."

"I'd be obliged," I said.

He gave me a long, slow look, then tipped his hat to Phoebe, and said, "Ma'am."

Phoebe nodded, and Hollis turned and walked away.

CHAPTER 6

THE TALL, LANKY kid had on a silly lookin' hat.

"You Emmett Love?" he said.

"I am."

"You can't have our whores," he said.

He must a'been waitin' for me to show up, since I'd only got ten feet inside Shingle's Dance Hall before he stepped in front of me.

"You can keep all them that want to stay," I said.

"They *all* wanna stay."

A few locals edged around us, close enough to hear, but far enough so they could jump out the way if bullets started flyin'.

I said, "Wanna bet?"

"Huh?"

"I bet you five dollars at least two whores will want to come with me."

He stiffened. "Guess we'll never know, will we?"

"Not 'til I ask 'em," I said.

He gave me a squint-eyed look and said, "I heard you're the best rifleman in Missouri. That true?"

"Probably."

"Better than Vince Tuttle?"

"I don't know Mr. Tuttle."

"Well, Vince Tuttle can shoot the hair off a gnat's ass."

"No shit?"

"No shit."

I nodded. "Well then, yeah, I'm better than Vince Tuttle."

"You don't know the man, how can you say that?"

"Vince may be hittin' gnat hair, but trust me, he's shootin' at gnat. If I'm shootin' gnat, there'll be gnat for supper."

There was chucklin' all around us, and the tall, lanky kid's face turned red. He said, "Even if you're the best rifleman in all creation it don't matter."

"It don't?"

"Nope."

"Why's that?"

He pointed at the six gun in my holster and smiled. "'Cause you ain't carryin' one."

"Well, it's hard to swing a rifle around a bar and shoot all three of you at the same time."

"What three?"

"You, the guy sittin' at the table with the pocket watch in front of him, and the guy hidin' upstairs, behind me."

"You can't even *see* him!"

"Don't need to, son. This is what I do."

He puffed his chest up a bit. "It's what *I* do, too. And anyways, I don't need my cousins to back my play if it's just you 'n me with handguns."

"Been practicin', have you?"

"I have."

"Around the farm?"

His face reddened again.

"Ain't no shame in that," I said. "Every great shootist I ever met started on a farm or ranch, shootin' fruit, vegetables, cans, and varmints."

He nodded.

I said, "You hittin' most of them apples and squashes you set on your fence post?"

"I hit all of 'em," he said, proudly. "Ever' time. And from different range."

"You pretty fast?" I said.

He smiled. "You can try me, you want."

"How much they payin' you here?"

"That's none a' your business."

"Reason I ask, if you're *really* good with a handgun, I might have a use for you."

He seemed surprised. "You'd take me with you?"

"Far as Springfield, anyway."

He looked around. Then, in a quiet voice he said, "How much you payin'?"

"You got a good horse?"

"Damn good horse."

"Any good with a rifle?"

He paused. "Not like you."

"You own one?"

He looked down. "Naw."

I nodded. "That's okay. Ten dollars."

"Ten dollars for two days work?"

"That's right. Ever been to Springfield?"

"Naw."

"It's a big town. Lotta bars. Bouncin' pays a dollar a day, free room and board. Wanna make more, try minin' in Colorado, or pannin' gold out west."

"What about hired gun work?"

"No offense, son, but you're not ready."

"You ain't seen me slap leather."

"True. But we been standin' here almost five minutes and you still ain't seen the derringer in my left hand."

He looked at the gun, but didn't twitch 'til I cocked it. A light bead of sweat formed on his upper lip.

"What kind of pansy-assed shootist carries a derringer?" he said.

"A live one."

He swallowed before speakin'. But he did speak.

"You know the job you was talkin' about just now?"

"Yeah?"

"I'll take it."

I nodded. "Good choice. What's your name, son?"

"Ira Glass."

"I'll be in touch, then, Mr. Glass."

He stood aside and let me pass.

CHAPTER 7

"WHAT'S IT LIKE," Scarlett said. "Really."

When Billy Shingles found he couldn't keep me from talkin' to his whores, he asked if I'd pay for an hour of their time. That seemed a fair request, so I gave him six dollars, and he let me talk to Scarlett and two others in Scarlett's bedroom. Billy knew he had no legal right to force the women to work for him, but he wasn't above tryin'. 'Course, Billy knew he had a gold mine in Rolla, this bein' the drop off point for every unmarried woman headin' west by railroad. So what if he lost a few girls every now and then? He'd still have an endless supply of new ones to take their place.

"There's five levels of whorin' out west," I said, answering Scarlett's question. "You don't need to worry about the top one."

"Why not?" said Gentry.

They were all sittin' on the bed. Gentry was slim of body, and wide-faced, with wide-set green eyes and long brown hair. Her face was littered with pimples, and scars from pimples that had come and gone. She could pass for twenty-two, but I figured her closer to eighteen. Scarlett was a big-boned gal from New Orleans, with wide hips and a gigantic bosom. Scarlett knew enough French to communicate with the third woman, Monique, who was twenty, French, and spoke practically no English. Because French-speakin' people were so rare in this part of the country, it was thought that wherever Scarlett went, Monique would follow.

Of the three, Monique was the looker.

"Well, the top whores like Lola Montez, are fine as cream gravy," I said. "Lola bathes in champagne every day, and wipes her butt with rose petals."

"Rose petals?" Gentry said. "Honest? Wow! I'd love to meet *her*!"

Scarlett said, "If you do, maybe she'll let you wipe your ass with the thorns."

"Well anyway," I said, "them type a' whores are what you call courtesans. Denver, Seattle, San Francisco—that's pretty much it. The next level is your parlor house whore, where they have a madam and professor. The professor's a piano player. They serve you and your gentleman food and drinks and then he'll ask if you want to go for a walk."

"A walk?" Gentry said.

"That means upstairs, to your bedroom."

"The music, food, and drink part sounds good," Gentry said.

"Well, it's somethin' to shoot for."

Scarlett said, "We heard tell you're honest, Mr. Love."

"I reckon I am," I said.

"Then be completely honest with us."

"Ma'am?"

"We need to know what to expect when we get there."

We looked at each other a minute, and then I said, "I s'pect Monique will land in one a' them parlor houses."

"But not us?"

While I thought about how to answer her question, Scarlett whispered to Monique, and patted her knee, reassuringly. Scarlett was no beauty, but she appeared to have a good heart.

"How old are you?" I said.

"Twenty-six," Scarlett said.

To Gentry I said, "I mean no offense, but are you pimply all over?"

"Just my face and the back of my neck."

"Your figure's good."

She smiled.

I said, "Any rashes, birth marks or scars?"

"No. I can show you, if you like."

I held up my hand. "Not necessary. I'm just thinkin' it through."

We all sat quiet a minute. Then I said, "I'll try to get the two of you with Mama Priss."

"Who's that?" said Gentry.

"Priscilla Bright. She's a madam, a friend of mine. She runs your next level of whorin', what they call a brothel."

"Like here," Scarlett said.

"Not this nice," I said. "You'll make your own food, do your own laundry, and buy your own clothes. But you'll make ten times the money."

"How's that possible?"

"There's a lot of money comes through Dodge, and women are scarce. One miner rode eighty miles to get a pancake breakfast from one of Priss's girls. Another was so homesick he walked thirty miles just to hold a woman's baby. What I'm sayin', if you nurture 'em, these men'll pay you ten dollars for a poke, and twenty-five for an overnight."

"Jesus!" Gentry said. "How much of that do we get to keep?"

"Half."

Monique whispered somethin' to Scarlett. Scarlett said, "How much will Monique get?"

"Monique's high end," I said. "She'll fetch a hundred a night."

Scarlett's eyes went big as saucers. She whispered it to Monique, and the pretty girl's face broke into a wide grin. She patted her crotch and then kissed the hand that did the pattin'. I kept watchin', waitin' to see what might happen next. But Gentry touched my leg to get my attention.

"If we don't land with Mama Priss, what's left?" said Gentry.

"Well, I'll get you on with Priss," I said.

"How old can we be to work there?" said Scarlett.

"If you take care of yourself, you've got 'til thirty-five at the brothel."

"Then what?"

"If you saved enough money, you can move somewhere else, become a proper woman, and start a restaurant, laundry or boardin' house."

"And if not?"

"Well, if you ain't saved your money or got married by then, you'll be hat-snatchers."

"What's that mean?"

"You'll live in a one-room shack or a tent in a minin' camp. When a prosperous-lookin' man walks by, you'll jump out and snatch his hat. He'll chase you to your place, and you'll try to coax him into a poke for whatever he'll pay. You can make a decent wage, but it's dangerous, 'cause you're on your own."

"And after that?"

"I won't lie to you, it ain't no easy life. Even with Mama Priss, you're gonna have no proper friends, and you won't be allowed in any of the better places, includin' most stores. You'll be shunned by proper women and served by no one. You'll hope to marry one a' your regulars or save enough money to open your own brothel."

"And if we don't?"

"Well, if you lose your looks, your health, and your money, the last stop is a hog ranch. That's a roadside buildin' on a stagecoach route or cattle trail in the middle of nowhere that you'll share with a dozen broke down alcoholic, drugged-out whores. If you wind up there, that's where you'll die."

"Wow!" Gentry said, pretendin' to be excited. "Sounds great! Won't Mum and Papa be proud when I introduce them to my friends at the hog ranch!"

I took another look at this gal, Gentry, and liked what I saw.

"You're fun," I said.

She flashed a pretty smile, then winked.

"You know it," she said.

CHAPTER 8

MY NEXT STOP was Lick and Casey's Dance Hall, where I met a feisty one-eyed whore named Mary Burns, and three others, Hester, Emma, and Leah. Unlike Mary, Hester had two eyes, but they were different colors, black and brown. Emma wore a pink ribbon in her hair, and had a distractin' way of fondlin' her breasts whenever she spoke. It took me no time at all to realize that while she had ten fingers all together, six of 'em were on one hand. Leah was thin as a rail and had a scar that ran from the corner of her eye to the side of her nose. It appeared to be a knife wound that had been poorly stitched. This was a ragged bunch of whores, whose ages ranged from south of eighteen to north of thirty. Most of their questions centered on the trip.

"We'll ride on horseback to Springfield," I said, "and take buckboards the rest of the way."

The women looked at each other.

Emma said, "We ain't got horses."

"You'll get some," I said.

"Where?"

"You'll buy'em."

"How?"

"With whatever money you've got, or by sellin' your possessions."

"How much luggage can we take?" Mary said.

"No more than a kit and saddlebags."

"What about our dresses?"

"If you can fit one in your kit, fine. Otherwise, no."

"How should we dress for the trip?" Leah said.

"Like men. And you'll be carryin' rifles and shotguns, even if you don't know how to use 'em."

"Are you insane?"

"My job is to get you to Dodge City, unless you decide to settle somewhere else along the way. But if you're in open country, wearin' women's clothin', your chances of gettin' to Dodge are poor. Between Indians, outlaws, soldiers, cowboys and renegades, you're pretty much bug meat. There'll be no perfume or powder in the Ozarks 'cause of bears, or on the Kansas plains, 'cause of Indians. I'll make you roll around in mud a few times, and rub dirt in your hair a time or two to keep the scent down."

"My friends went west," Mary said. "And they didn't have to do all that. They wore their finest clothes and perfumes the whole way."

"You should a' gone with your friends," I said, "or wait 'til the next bunch goes. 'Cause right now there's a major draught in Kansas. Thirty thousand men are on the trails, lookin' for water. Dodge City's still wet, but most of central and east Kansas is dry, and some men there'll kill you for your canteen. By dressin' like men, carryin' guns, we'll have a show of force. At least we'll appear to, from a distance."

"I heard you're bringing a mail-order bride," Emma said.

"Word travels fast."

She shrugged. "It's Rolla."

"She gonna ride in the buckboard with us?" Hester asked.

"At some point she probably will."

"Does she know it?"

"Not yet."

"Can I be there when you tell her?"

I grinned. "Nope."

CHAPTER 9

I HAD A drink at Lick and Casey's, then got a room on the second floor of the Mountain View Hotel, overlookin' Main Street. After stowin' my gear, I chose a corner table in the hotel restaurant and ordered a beefsteak. It was early yet, and the other customers were seated on the far side of the room, at the bar, with their backs to me. The waiter left to place my order, and I settled into my seat, thinkin', *this is how life ought to be!* No gun hands, no drunken cowboys spoilin' for a fight, no quick-draw kids tryin' to make their reps off me. I'd enjoy a good steak, some beans and taters, a couple drinks, and get a good night's sleep in a real bed with clean sheets. No ticks, spiders, snakes or scorpions to worry over. In the mornin' I'd have a hot bath, shave, and haircut while they wash my laundry. Then what, maybe ask Phoebe Thayer to lunch? That was a happy thought.

A young lady entered the restaurant, looked in my direction, hesitated, then approached my table. She seemed nervous.

"Mr. Love?"

"Yes?"

"I'm Jenny Palmer. May I sit with you a moment?"

"You may. Can I buy you dinner?"

"That's very kind of you, but no. I have business to discuss."

I nodded at the chair across from me. She looked around the room before takin' it, and when she sat, she scooted as close to the table as she could get.

"How can I help you, Miss Palmer?"

She placed an envelope on the table between us, and said, "Are you familiar with a town called Grand Junction?"

"Never been there, but I heard of it," I said. "Heard they got a new stagecoach."

"That's right."

There was no one within hearin' distance, but she lowered her voice anyway. "Last year I began corresponding with a man named Roy Ellsworth, who has a ranch four miles south of there. In April, my friend Sophie and I took the first stage from Kansas City to Grand Junction."

"How'd you get to Kansas City?"

"We took the train from St. Louis."

"That weren't cheap."

"My father paid our fare."

She went quiet a minute.

I said, "Then what happened?"

"The purpose of my trip was to meet Mr. Ellsworth, to see if there might be a marital connection between us."

"Your friend went with you?"

Jenny nodded. "Sophie felt if I could find love there, perhaps she could, too. We've always been best friends, and thought it would be grand if the two of us could marry men who lived close to each other. We had dreams of raising our children on neighboring ranches. I suppose that sounds silly to you."

"Not at all. Sounds like a well-thought plan."

She looked at the envelope on the table.

I said, "How'd you hear about this man, Ellsworth?"

"He bought space in the St. Louis Daily Herald, and advertised himself as a lonely rancher who wanted a wife with whom to share his ranch and the dreams of his heart."

"You trusted a flannel-mouth man like that?"

"In retrospect, I concede I was terribly gullible."

I only understood half the words she used, but figured something bad must a' took place. I said, "What happened when you got there?"

She paused. "If I speak frankly, will you agree to keep my confidence?"

"If you're askin' will I repeat what you tell me, the answer is no. You have my word on that."

Jenny bit her lip. "Mr. Ellsworth met our stage on Thursday, April twelfth, and offered to take us to his ranch in a mule-drawn wagon. He must have imbibed a portion of whiskey while waiting for us at the depot, because we smelled it on his breath. But he seemed in control of his faculties, and Sophie and I had been traveling three days, and were eager to see the ranch, so we agreed to accompany him there. It was early afternoon and we figured to see the place, inspect the kitchen, bedrooms, outhouse and livestock, and hoped for a nice chat. Then, if he had the fixings, I'd cook him a nice dinner. Afterward, he'd take us back to town where Sophie and I planned to spend the night at the Holland House on Main Street."

"But that didn't work out, did it?"

She sighed. "Unfortunately, Mr. Ellsworth consumed an additional quantity of whiskey en route to his ranch. By the time we arrived, he was in a vile state. He cursed us, cuffed us about with his fists, and took our money."

Jenny had a pleasant mouth that moved more than it needed to when formin' words, and my eyes were drawn to it as she spoke. But when her lower lip quivered slightly, I asked, "Anythin' else happen?"

She lowered her eyes. "He...attempted to despoil us."

I waited a few seconds. Then said, "And did he?"

Jenny's voice wavered as she spoke her story.

"Thanks to Sophie's presence and the grace of God, Mr. Ellsworth failed to sully our virtue, though he made every attempt to do so. He finally passed out drunk, and we took that opportunity to escape."

I nodded. "When he passed out, why didn't you take back the money he stole?"

"We wanted to, but it was in his pockets, and we were afraid he might stir."

"Did you tell all this to the sheriff?"

"On our way back to town we came upon a ranch. The woman who lived there drove us to the depot in her buggy.

We implored her to take us to the sheriff, but she claimed there was no sheriff in Grand Junction, and the Marshall was fifty miles away. Upon hearing our story, the stagecoach proprietor refunded our money and gave us a courtesy ride back to Kansas City."

"Probably didn't want any bad publicity for his new business," I said.

The waiter approached and asked Jenny if she'd care for a drink. She declined, and he left after tellin' me my steak would be ready soon.

"What's in the envelope?" I said.

"Sixty-eight dollars."

"What's it for?"

"I want you to kill Roy Ellsworth."

"Excuse me?"

"Sophie and I would be obliged if you'd send that drunken reprobate to Hell. Pardon my language."

"Why come to me with this?"

"Most everyone in town knows your reputation."

"You think I kill people for money?"

"I can only hope so."

"Grand Junction is forty miles outta my way. Makin' it an eighty mile trip."

"I have reason to believe Mr. Ellsworth has a considerable sum of money in a large trunk under his bed."

"And you want me to share it with you?"

"Of course not! How could you even suggest such a thing?"

"My apologies, Miss."

She stared at me a minute, then said, "I only meant there could be a larger financial benefit for you than the contents of this envelope."

"I meant no insult, Miss."

"That's all right," she said. "I understand why you asked the question."

"I have another, if it won't offend you," I said.

"Please feel free to ask it."

"How did you come by this knowledge of a trunk full of money under his bed?"

"While drunk, Mr. Ellsworth shouted, 'you're only here for my money!' We protested, but he told us never to enter his bedroom, or he'd cut off our heads and put them in the trunk under his bed."

"That must have scared the shit outta you!"

She raised an eyebrow.

"Sorry, Miss. I don't have town manners. That's probably no secret."

"In truth," she said, "I'm quite impressed with your manners. You haven't spit or broken wind in my presence and this is the first hint of a curse. If you remember, I cursed too, just a moment ago."

I nodded and looked her over. Jenny wasn't a short girl, but she sat short. Her posture was good, so I figured she had uncommon long legs. Her face was bland and mostly clear-complected, and her nose was straight. Aside from bein' the type of woman who'd pay to have a man killed, I didn't see anythin' in Jenny's looks or manner that'd lead Mr. Ellsworth to attack and rob her and Sophie. As a former shootist, I learned early on to watch a man's eyes when he spoke, 'less he was playin' cards, and if he was, I'd study his mouth. A gambler will control his eyes, but it's hard to guard your eyes and mouth at the same time.

Unless you're a woman.

In my experience, watchin' a woman's eyes and mouth means nothin'. I never know if they're truthful or lyin', which is one of the reasons I travel with a witchy twenty-year-old gal named Rose. Tiny as she is, Rose can drive a wagon and put a camp together good as any man. She also does curious things that can't be explained, like climbin' tall trees with wide trunks that have no low branches. And talkin' to horses. And smellin' tubers and medicine roots below the ground, and sniffin' truth above it. Rose could hear the first words of a story like this from a woman like Jenny and know if it's true, partly true, or untrue. But Rose was in Springfield with the wagons, and I was on my own with Jenny's story. I had no reason to doubt it, and she seemed honest. But the whole money under the bed part stuck in my craw.

"How'd you come by this odd sum?" I said.

"Sophie and I saved it from our jobs."

"What type of work you do?"

"Sophie works in her father's general store, and I work at Miss Patty's. That's how I learned you were in town."

"You met Phoebe at Miss Patty's?"

"Yes, and she announced you were taking her to Newton. Are you?"

I nodded.

"In that case, will you consider making a short detour to Mr. Ellsworth's ranch, south of Grand Junction? Though dusty, the trails are flat and easy to follow."

I knew that to be mostly true.

"You saved sixty-eight dollars since April?" I asked.

"The amount includes a small weekly stipend I get from my father, and birthday money, and the sale of the gold watch Sophie's father left her."

"You girls have worked up a mighty big rage to want the man killed."

"I fear for the next poor girl who answers his advertisement. She may fare worse."

We saw the waiter making his way across the room with my platter of steak. Jenny stood.

"What say you to my offer, Mr. Love?"

"I'll think on it," I said. "But keep your envelope."

"Consider it expense money."

I handed her the envelope, then signaled the waiter to stay where he was, so we could have a moment of privacy. When he did, I looked Jenny in the eye and lowered my voice.

"I don't take money to kill people," I said. "If a man needs killin', I'll oblige him. But money don't enter into it."

She nodded.

"How much did Roy Ellsworth steal from you and Sophie?"

"Sixty-eight dollars."

"Now there's a coincidence," I said.

CHAPTER 10

PHOEBE WASN'T THRILLED about travelin' the woods and plains with a pack of whores, but she was—what's the word Rose says? Philisofgul? If that's the word, Phoebe was that. About it.

"They have as much right to go west as I do," she said.

"They do," I agreed.

"I don't know much about soiled doves," Phoebe said, "but I feel for their plight."

"What plight is that?"

"Living the way they do."

I wondered what she could possibly know about how whores live. She caught my look of curiosity, and said, "Do they not live in fear of disease? And danger?"

"They do. And loneliness."

The look in her face told me she hadn't thought about that part.

"One thing about whores of a proper age," I said. "They know what they're gettin' into."

"On the other hand," Phoebe said, "I've heard dreadful stories about minors being forced into prostitution."

"That's crazy," I said. In my experience, miners love whores even more than cowboys do! Only politicians love 'em more–"

"Not miners, you dolt. Minors."

"Ma'am?"

"Girls as young as twelve."

"Oh. Well, twelve ain't a problem out west."

"What?" She seemed shocked.

"Twelve is legal marryin' age for girls," I said. "Though them that are forced to marry a grown man at twelve are often treated worse than whores."

"Well, that's appalling."

"Out west the age of consent is ten."

"*Ten?* Are you serious?"

"Sheriffs don't get involved 'less a girl's under ten. 'Less she's been beaten."

"How can a ten year old girl be expected to provide consent?"

"I can't explain the why's and wherefores. I'm just sayin' how it works out west."

"These women I'll be traveling with," Phoebe said. "Are they dangerous?"

I thought about sayin' all women were dangerous, but I knew what she meant. So I said, "Never steal from a whore, or accuse one of stealin'."

She looked amused. "If you're giving me a list, why would you think to put that first?"

"'Cause whores don't steal. They're the most honest people on earth."

"I've never heard that, and frankly, I don't believe it."

"Well, I don't know about the whores back East," I said. "But out west, miners give nuggets and gold dust to their favorite whores for safekeepin'."

"What if another—ah guest—enters her room and steals it?"

"Well, that'd come under the headin' of never steal from a whore. That man's a goner."

"Mr. Love, a moment ago you informed me that some of these prostitutes are ten years old. How shall I expect to believe they could kill a grown man?"

"Whores know a hundred ways to kill a man. Poison's common, but so are knives, guns, customers, and other whores. Not sayin' it's impossible to rob a whore and live, but if a man does, he'll always be lookin' over his shoulder, even if he moves away."

"Why?"

"'Cause whores move too, from camp to camp and town to town. Their customers are mostly miners and cowboys, so everyone moves in the same circles. You steal from a whore in Laramie, she'll find you in Medicine Bow, or Bitter Creek."

"It appears you know quite a lot about these sorts of women."

I shook my head. "Ma'am, I don't know a lot about *any* sorts of women."

She enjoyed a short laugh. Then said, "Apart from stealing, is there anything else I should know?"

"Whores' dresses have pockets that work from the inside. They keep daggers and derringers and vials of poison in 'em. You don't want to strike a whore, because some are ill-tempered, and all are tougher than they look."

Phoebe seemed amused. "Anything else?"

"They fight dirty."

She laughed again. "I'll keep that in mind in case I ever find myself in a boxing match with a prostitute."

I nodded. "In general, it ain't wise to mess with whores."

"I can assure you I won't 'mess' with them, as you put it. My interest is strictly peaceful coexistence for the duration of the trip."

I stared at her blankly.

She said, "I want us all to get along."

"We'll get along when we have to," I said.

"Well, why wouldn't we?"

"They can be a sharp-tongued lot."

"Meaning?"

"You don't cotton to cussin'."

"I make no secret of my stance on profanity."

"Well ma'am, whores can cuss to make *me* blush."

"You're joking."

"I'm not. And you'll be wise to pretend you can't hear 'em."

"Why on earth would I do that?"

"If they know it bothers you, they'll do it twice as much."

Phoebe frowned. "They sound like an antagonistic lot."

"Don't know what that means," I said. "But it ain't always good to mix whores with proper women."

"Why not?"

I struggled to put my thoughts into words. "There are certain types of behavior you consider improper and unladylike."

"Of course. What of it?"

"Well, them things don't affect whores the same way."

Phoebe looked uneasy, but spoke no more on the subject.

CHAPTER 11

I HAD TO produce my gun in a quick fashion to the liveryman for sellin' Gentry a lame horse.

"That were a legal transaction," he said. "You can't just come in here and threaten to shoot me!"

Gentry stood slightly behind me, holdin' her new horse by the lead attached to its halter. I cocked the hammer on my Colt.

"You wouldn't!" he said.

"I never pull my weapon," I said. "Less I intend to use it."

"What about the Sheriff?"

"Hollis'll shoot you too, if I happen to miss."

"What?"

"You don't sell a lame horse to a lady," I said. "Specially one that's travelin' the Ozarks."

"A *lady?*" He relaxed a bit, pointed at Gentry. "She ain't no lady, Mr. Love. Why, that's little Gentry from Shingles. She's a whore."

I'd had enough. "Defend yourself or I'll shoot you where you stand."

He tensed up again. "There's witnesses," he said.

He meant his wife and the kid who stacks his hay. They were standin' frozen where they'd stood when I first entered the livery. Neither had spoken. I figured the boy hoped I wouldn't shoot his boss and the wife hoped I would.

"Your choice," I said, evenly.

He looked at his wife and hay stacker. "I'll give her a different horse."

"And five dollars extra."

His face turned red.

"It's all right, Emmett," Gentry said. "I don't want to cause any trouble."

"She's a *whore!*" he said, spittin' the word at me.

I cuffed him with the back of my gloved hand, and the rawhide ridges on it sliced his cheek. A line of blood formed. He touched it with his palm and stared at it.

"You got no right," he said.

"Five dollars," I repeated. "And a true horse. And an apology."

He was mad as a hornet, but he replaced her horse and gave Gentry the five dollars. I didn't move, nor holster my gun. It took him a minute to realize what I was waitin' for.

Through clenched teeth, he said, "I'm sorry, Mr. Love."

"The apology ain't for me," I said. "It's for Gentry."

"I ain't apologizin' to no whore," he said. "Go ahead and shoot me, and fuck you both!"

"You *will* apologize, or Gentry and your missus'll have a little chat about you right here and now."

He glared at Gentry like his eyes were deadly weapons.

"I apologize, Miss," he said.

Gentry walked over to him. The look on her face said she was sorry for what she'd put him through. But then she kicked his nuts with her steel-toed boot, and he crumpled to his knees in agony. I thought she might kick him again, but he vomited, and she backed off. Gentry looked at his wife, and said, "If that'll keep him off you a week, I reckon' I done you a favor."

The wife spit the ground in Gentry's direction, and we left with the new horse.

CHAPTER 12

WE SLIPPED OUT of town at four a.m., after remindin' everyone we'd be leavin' six hours later. That way the liveryman and his friends—and Billy Shingles and his friends—wouldn't be waitin' outside of town to ambush us.

We rode single file with me in front, Phoebe second. Six of the whores shared the next three horses, followed by Scarlett, who rode a mule. Bringin' up the rear was Ira Glass, the tall, lanky kid who tried to keep me from enterin' Shingles Dance Hall a few nights earlier.

The women wore buckskin breeches, and cotton shirts with leather jackets in different shades of brown. Scarlett wore a vest under her coat to help flatten her chest. We all had on cowboy hats, except Ira, who sported a bowler with a dome crown, leather sweatband, and ribbon trim. To Phoebe I muttered, "That type a'hat would look good on a chief's lodge pole."

The six-mile point of our journey put us a short distance from a bend of the Gasconade, where I expected to find five stones by the side of the trail. But there were only four, which gave me pause until I figured what was up.

"Okay," I said. "We'll stop here and rest the horses a mite."

"Can we eat now?" Emma said.

"Sit tight. I'll fetch somethin'."

"What should I do?" Ira said.

"Build us a fire and keep an eye on the ladies. I'll be back directly."

As the women dismounted, I steered Major through a thicket toward the place Shrug and I like to fish. This part of the river has so many twists and turns, it takes fourteen miles by water to cover three miles by land. When I got there, I found ten perch hangin' from a tree branch.

I stopped and waited.

When the rock exploded against a tree three feet from my head I didn't even flinch.

"Hey, Shrug," I said.

He popped out from behind a tree, scamperin' low and crablike, pointin' and grinnin' at me. Then he pointed at Major.

"We're both used to the rocks," I said.

Shrug nodded.

I dismounted, and tied Major's rein to a low bush so he could graze. Shrug moved toward Major, lifted one of his back legs, and removed a pebble from his hoof. Then he gave me a look that said I should a' known about the pebble.

"Kiss my ass," I said. Then added, "Thanks."

He looked at my saddlebags.

"Left side," I said.

He grinned like a kid with candy and reached into the saddlebag. When he found the bottle of bourbon his smile got bigger.

"That's genuine Kentucky bourbon," I said. "All the way from Louisville."

Shrug cocked his head.

I said, "The Mountain View Hotel gets it shipped by rail twice a month."

He nodded approvingly.

"Hell of an age we live in, ain't it?"

He shrugged.

"It's yours," I said. "Enjoy."

Shrug worked the cork out and took a pull. He smiled broadly, fell on his back, and kicked his legs in the air. Shrug loves his whiskey. He came up grinnin' and took another pull.

"Go easy, friend," I said. "It's smooth goin' down, but it will flat kick your ass."

He took another pull and pointed at the fish.

"That's ten perch," I said. "You're not joinin' us for breakfast?"

He shook his head and kissed his bottle of bourbon.

I pointed at the saddlebags.

"There's a leather pouch in there, with matches in a wax rag, and a couple blocks of salt. Got some salt pork, too, and chitlins."

His eyes grew big.

"Yup, chitlins. Can you believe it?"

Shrug pretended to swoon. He pulled the saddlebag off Major and dug out his prizes. Shrug don't have much use for money, but I'd put a few gold and silver coins in his pouch anyway.

"Anythin' else I can do for you?" I said.

He sniffed the air.

I laughed. "I'll see what I can do."

He made a curvy motion with his hands. Then closed his eyes and kissed the air.

"Monique. She's French."

He gave me a questionin' look. I said, "Don't get your hopes up."

Shrug pretended to pout. I laughed.

"Maybe Scarlett," I said.

He cocked his head.

"Big gal in the back. She's got a good heart."

He put his hands out in front of him and grinned.

"Yeah, they're huge all right!"

His expression turned sad. He circled his hand in front of his face.

"Gentry," I said. "I'm partial to her."

He cocked his head again.

I said, "Her face don't bother me. She's got grit. I like that in a woman."

Shrug raised his eyebrows.

"It'll be up to her," I said. "I don't know. We'll see."

He put the saddlebags back on Major, then picked up his new pouch, tied it to his belt, grabbed his bottle, and scampered off into the bushes. When I got back to camp with the fish, only Phoebe had a clue as to how I'd come by 'em, and she kept it to herself. Ira, in particular, was mystified.

"What kind a' bait did you use?"

"Words."

"What?"

"I talked 'em out of the river and told 'em to lay still on the bank while I strung 'em up."

Gentry giggled. Mary rolled her eyes.

"No one can talk to fish," Ira said.

"My friend Rose can speak to all species of fish," I said, while filletin' Shrug's catch. "But I only speak perch and catfish."

After breakfast we followed the stones to Limestone Pass, where the ridin' turned slow and treacherous. The women in the middle had to alternate ridin' and walkin' down the steep trail that took us to the base of Skull Mountain. Along the way, I pointed out a row of caves to Phoebe.

"See them caves?" I said. "There's more than fifteen hundred of 'em in this county, and half belong to bears. You were damn lucky to find an empty one."

She raised an eyebrow at my curse, but let it slide.

At the base of Skull Mountain, we found a stream to water our horses and fill our canteens. With that done, I said, "Ladies, this is a good place to relieve yourselves. Pair up and find a bush if you want, but don't go more than fifty feet in any direction."

Ira and I pissed on the far side of our horses, so as not to offend Phoebe, but the whores shucked their drawers, squatted, and pissed right where they stood. I could tell Phoebe was workin' hard to keep the emotions off her face.

Scarlett saw it, too. After pissin', she moved slowly toward Phoebe.

"I'll go with you to the bushes, Ma'am, if you care to."

Phoebe hesitated a moment, then said, "Thank you. That's very kind of you."

Mary called out, "I shoulda known Miss Fancy Pants was too good to piss with the rest of us."

Leah hollered, "Tell us what her drawers look like, Scarlett!"

"Probably got lace and gold dust wove into 'em," someone said.

Emma and Hester were gigglin' and snickerin' about somethin' they'd said quietly to each other, and I thought, *this is gonna be a long trip.*

CHAPTER 13

THE HAMMER OF a .36 caliber Colt Revolvin' Belt Pistol makes a unique sound when cocked.

I heard that sound just before dawn, and had to force myself not to jerk up. I opened my eyes to find the shadowy outline of Ira Glass drawin' a bead on me from point blank range. I had my derringer in my right hand under the blanket, as I always did when sleepin', and my .44 Colt Army pistol beside my leg. But I'd have to cock it before firin', and wouldn't have time to do that if Ira fired first.

"You don't seem so high 'n mighty now, do you, Emmett Love?"

"Maybe not to you," I said. "Maybe not at this partic'lar moment."

"I could shoot you where you lie," he said. "Just kill you right now."

"Why don't you then?"

"You don't mean that."

"The hell I don't. It'd save me havin' to hear all your thoughts while you work up the courage."

"Shootin' you would make me the most famous gunman in this part of the country. You know that?"

"I'm much more famous out west. Why don't you wait and shoot me there?"

He started to speak, but died before the words got past his lips.

"*Mon Dieu!*" Monique shrieked. "*Putain qu'est-ce qui s'est passé?*"

I sat up and leaned over his body and felt for a pulse.

"Ira caught a stray rock," I said.

"He *what?*" Gentry said.

"A rock came flyin' into camp and hit poor Ira in the head."

"Is he dead?"

"Feels like it."

"I mean, does that happen often?" she said. "Are there likely to be more rocks flying into camp?"

"Usually there's just the one."

The women gathered close to me.

"Do you think he would have shot you?" Emma said.

"I do for a fact."

"Lucky that rock flew into camp, then," Scarlett said.

"What do we do now?" Phoebe said.

I looked at the horizon. "There's less than an hour before dawn. We should get what sleep we can."

I laid back down and closed my eyes, but no one else made a move for their bed rolls.

"What about Ira?" Leah said.

"Least he ain't snorin'," Scarlett said.

"Well, I can't sleep with a dead man in camp," Gentry said.

"I was stuck under a dead man for more'n a hour once," Hester said.

"You mean Mike Pike?" Mary said. "Big fat guy that died a couple years ago?"

"Uh huh."

"I would've screamed," Mary said.

"You think I didn't?" Hester said. "I screamed bloody murder."

"And no one came to help you?" Phoebe said.

I sat up, surprised to hear her voice among the whores. Hester said, "No one came 'cause they thought I was pretendin' to be in the throes of rapture."

"Helluva way to die," I said.

"Spoken like a man," Hester said.

Instead of sleepin', we huddled together and talked. When it got light enough to see detail, I was mildly surprised to find two death wounds on Ira's head.

Phoebe pulled me away from the others and said, "Wayne did that?"

"Yup."

"But how?"

"I told you he's an uncommon good rock chucker."

"You expect me to believe he hurled a large stone at this man's head, in the dark, and hit it, and then threw another so quickly and accurately that he hit him a second time? Before Ira had time to fall down?"

"Less you got a better explanation, that's how I see it," I said.

"Well, that's preposterous!" Phoebe exclaimed.

"Is that some sort of fancy cuss word?"

"No. But what Monique said earlier was reprehensible."

"Wait–you speak French?"

"And Spanish, and Latin, if you care to know."

"Not many folks speak Latin around here," I said.

She paused. "Well, no, of course not."

"Maybe you can teach 'em to speak it in Newton," I said, helpfully.

She gave out a sigh of exasperation.

"No one actually *speaks* Latin," she said.

"Oh. I thought you said you did."

She closed her eyes and took a deep breath. "Let's just forget the Latin part, shall we?"

"Okay."

I saddled my horse. "Can I ask you about the French words Monique said?"

"I'll not repeat them, if that's what you mean."

"No need. It's just that those are the first words she spoke the whole trip that I could hear."

"So?"

"I thought they sounded right beautiful."

"You *would*."

I put the rest of my gear on Major, slid my rifle into the scabbard, and looked around to see who needed the most help gettin' ready. Turned out to be Phoebe. While I helped her saddle her horse, I said, "Would you ever consider speakin' a few words of proper French to me?"

"Perhaps I should. Then maybe you and Wayne could communicate."

"What?" I was thunderstruck. "You sayin' Wayne–I mean, Shrug–speaks French?"

Three feet away, a piece of rock exploded for no apparent reason. Then I heard the gunshot that caused it and realized we were bein' attacked by Indians.

CHAPTER 14

"JESUS, WAKE THE snakes!" Gentry shouted.

"*Nous allons tous mourir!*" Monique screamed.

"Stop screamin'!" I yelled.

"Well, *you're* screaming!" Emma shouted.

Another bullet struck the dirt between Phoebe and me.

"Light a shuck for that overhang!" I yelled. "When you get there, squat down and tuck in deep to give 'em a smaller target. If they start shootin' from the other ridge, turn and run behind them rocks over yonder!"

Another shot landed near Gentry's horse.

"Scarlett!"

"Yes sir?"

"Help me get the horses under the trees. If they shoot our mounts, it'll be a long walk to Springfield."

"Yes sir!"

Five additional shots were fired as we got the horses under cover. I looked up to the crest of the western ridge and spotted four braves, and guessed there were probably a few more dug in among the crags and crevices.

"Scarlett, you'd best stay here," I said. "I'll draw their attention."

"I'll come with you, Emmett, if you need help."

I looked at the big-boned gal with the heart of gold who made her livin' by pleasurin' men, who, hours ago, had escorted Phoebe behind the rocks so she could piss proper. Now, here she was, offerin' to risk her life against maraudin' Indians.

"Scarlett," I said, "you're a helluva useful woman to have around."

"Thanks, Emmett."

A couple more shots hit the rocks around us. Scarlett was plenty scared, but fightin' to look brave. This was the type of woman that could help tame a rugged land.

"You're gonna make some lucky man a good wife," I said.

"Yippee," she said, without much enthusiasm.

She and I were with the horses on the east end of the camp, under a canopy of trees. The others were huddled under the overhang on the west end of camp, directly below the Indians. The open area between us measured about thirty yards. No one had been hit. Yet.

"Where's Wayne?" Phoebe shouted from her hidin' place on the other side of camp.

"Who's Wayne?" Gentry hollered.

"Shrug can't be everywhere at the same time," I shouted. "This is *our* party. Now hobble your lips, and don't distract me!"

I climbed on Major's back and pulled my Henry from the scabbard.

"Where are you *going*?" Leah wailed. "Don't you *dare* leave us!"

"*Shut up!*" I yelled.

I'd told 'em time and again I didn't want the Indians to know I was travelin' with eight women. Now their screamin' had ruined that.

Three more shots peppered the rocks around me. With rifle in hand, I spread my arms wide apart and shouted, "Fox Indians are weak! Their women have pox! They fornicate with dogs!"

Nothin'.

I went all in with the biggest insult possible: "Fox warriors clean the camp and take care of the children!"

Four Indians jumped to their feet, screamin' furiously, and I shot three of 'em. Then I shouted, "This is a forty-four caliber Henry Repeatin' Rifle. A resolute man, armed with one a' these, partic'larly on horseback, *cannot be captured!*"

They had no idea what I was talkin' about, but I'd read them words on the hand bill advertisin' the Henry Repeatin' Rifle, and liked the way they sounded.

"Look!" I shouted at the Indians. "I'm fearless. Shoot me! Do your best, but know I cannot be killed!"

There was no movement from the rocks, just the cries of two gut-shot Fox Indians bleedin' out. The third was either unconscious or dead. I heard some of 'em scramblin' about, attemptin' to transport the dyin' men without becomin' targets themselves.

"Go back to Iowa!" I shouted. "And take your dead with you!"

Their blood-curdlin' death sounds had reduced to moanin', but I continued shoutin' threats and oaths 'til I heard Shrug's whistle, tellin' me the danger had passed.

"You can come out now," I said to the women. "I'm sorry for yellin' at you."

"That was the bravest thing I ever seen!" Gentry cooed.

Scarlett noticed the way Gentry was eyeballin' me, and whispered, "Looks like you hooked one. But be careful reelin' her in tonight. She's a famous screamer."

The whores gathered round me and Major and expressed their gratitude. Phoebe held off expressin' her opinion 'til I'd buried Ira and gotten us miles away from the Indian attack.

"That was the most irresponsible behavior I have ever witnessed," she said. "You were daring those Indians to shoot you. And what if they had? Where would we be then? What would have become of us?"

"Why, Shrug would've taken you to Springfield," I said.

"It was a foolish, ill-thought thing to do."

"The others thought I was brave."

"You were foolish. You showed bad judgment, and could've been killed."

I laughed.

"What's so funny?"

"Them Indians couldn't have shot me, 'cept by accident."

"What do you mean?"

"Indians can't shoot for shit. Pardon the expression."

"I don't understand."

"They were usin' old muzzleloaders and single-shot rifles."

"I still don't understand."

"Their guns ain't accurate at that distance. They were shootin' straight out, hopin' the bullets would fall on our heads. They got no skill."

"How can that be true?"

"Well, they don't get much practice."

"Why not?"

"Ain't got bullets enough to practice. And even if they did, they got no tools to keep their guns oiled and cleaned. I'm surprised their rifles didn't blow up in their faces today."

I turned to glance at Phoebe and saw her face turnin' red.

"What?" I said.

She gestured behind her. "You accepted the women's accolades and pronouncements of bravery and gave them no accounting of the true nature of the events. Same as you did with the fish Wayne gave you yesterday. You're trying to falsely impress us, Emmett Love, and sadly, it seems to be working with the others."

"But not you."

"Of course not. I can spot counterfeit courage a mile away."

"Of course you can."

"But some cannot, especially the younger girls among us. And you're leading them to believe you're courageous and capable, when you're not."

"Well, I did happen to shoot three Indians."

"So?"

"Three hits in three seconds from low ground to high, sixty yards, on a skittish horse..."

"Your point, sir?"

"Some folks might be inclined to call that a right capable display of marksmanship."

"Oh, pooh!"

"Pooh?"

"You couldn't kill a rabbit last week with twenty minutes and a rifle. Wayne killed three with rocks. And yesterday Wayne had to catch your breakfast, and last night he saved your life. Had Wayne not intervened with Ira, you'd be dead today."

"So?"

"You're enjoying all the glory, and no one even knows about poor Wayne."

"Well, you do."

"That's right. And you should be ashamed."

"Why's that?"

"You've got these women cow-eyed and swooning over you. They're starting to think of you in heroic terms."

"What's wrong with that?"

"It's fraud."

I said, "Are you upset that Wayne wasn't there when the shootin' started?"

"I'm nothing of the sort. I'm sure he was tackling something much more dangerous."

"Uh huh."

"He rightfully assumed that even a person with your limited skills could vanquish a handful of teenage Indians with inadequate weaponry."

"And he speaks French, too," I said.

"He does. And beautifully, I might add."

I was riding in front of her, so she couldn't see me smile.

"Are you smiling?" Phoebe said.

I chose not to answer her.

"Are you smiling?" she repeated.

The sky overhead was clear and crisp, and Shrug was leadin' us away from the Indians I hadn't killed. We crested a flat-topped mountain and stopped to rest our horses. Those who needed to shit, did so behind rocks. The others squatted and pissed in plain view, which vexed Phoebe visibly.

"Monique," she said. "*Allez-vous m'escorter aux rochers?*"

"*Chier ou pisser, Mademoiselle?*"

"*Je préfèrerais que le monde entier ne sache pas quelles sont mes affaires derrière les rochers, si vous n'avez pas d'objection.*"

Monique and Scarlett laughed at whatever Phoebe had said, but Monique went with her behind the rocks.

While waitin' for 'em, I brushed a spider off my pant leg and took a moment to observe the natural order of things around me. I looked up and saw a hawk glidin' silently through the air toward a rock formation, some sixty yards distant. I followed its line of sight, and spotted a squirrel runnin' full speed along a ledge, headin' for a stand of bull pines. The hawk circled once, then swooped down and made off with its prize.

The squirrel never knew what hit it.

CHAPTER 15

AFTER THE REST stop I led the ladies to a muddy creek, and sighed, knowin' what to expect. For the women, this was usually the hardest part of the journey.

"I ain't fillin' my canteen with that shit water," Mary said.

"No one's askin' you to," I said.

"Then why are we stoppin'?"

"Dismount."

"*Qu'est-ce que ce fou à en vu pour nous maintenant?*" Monique said.

Scarlett said, "*Je ne sais pas. Il ne l'a pas dit.*"

"Climb down from your horses," I said.

"Why?" Leah said.

"We're gonna mud the scent off you."

"What?"

"I told you this back at Lick and Casey's."

"Well, you didn't tell me!" Phoebe said.

"Get your asses in the mud," I said. "All of you."

"I'll not do it," Phoebe said. "Not willingly."

I hoisted her on my shoulder and tossed her in the mud puddle and rolled her around 'til her hair, face, and clothin' were a muddy mess. She sputtered and spit, and slapped me when she could, but to her credit, she never cussed.

"Anyone else need a hand?" I said.

"What's the purpose of this?" Scarlett said.

"Yonder's bear country. This mud'll get the female scent off you."

"I ain't afraid," Hester said. "I've fucked a few bears in my time."

"Not like these," I said. "Look ladies, it's just mud. If it keeps you alive, what do you care? Just give me a chance to get you through this wild part of the country. You can wash your hair and clothes when we get to the White River."

"Where's that?" Gentry said.

"Twelve miles outta Springfield. We're campin' there tonight."

"You gonna talk more fish into the fryin' pan?" Gentry said.

"We'll see. In the meantime, get in the mud."

"With pleasure!" Gentry said.

She ran to the mud puddle full speed and dove into it on her stomach and slid nearly twenty feet. The others thought that looked like fun, so they joined in. Before long they were laughin' and rollin' around in the mud, and slappin' pads of it in each other's hair. It was such a comical scene, even Phoebe was smilin'.

Then Gentry said, “What about you, Emmett?”

Before I could protest or get away, all the whores squealed and ran toward me and dragged me into the puddle. They pushed and poked and rolled me around, and slapped my face with mud cakes, and laughed and giggled. But when it suddenly grew quiet, I noticed it was Gentry layin’ on top of me, kissin’ my cheeks and mouth.

The others backed away, silently.

“I like you, Emmett,” Gentry said.

“I’m honored,” I said. “But right now we need to get through some rough country.”

“Maybe we can get together tonight,” she said. “After we bathe in the White River?”

“A lot can happen ’tween now and then,” I said.

She smiled broadly.

“It sure can,” she said.

Though her mouth was covered with mud, Gentry’s teeth were sparklin’ white. I hadn’t remembered ’em bein’ so pretty the other times she’d smiled. As she climbed off me, she placed her hand on my privates by accident. Only the way she did it, didn’t feel so much like an accident. Then the way her hand sort of stayed there longer than it had to also didn’t feel like an accident.

But it didn’t feel bad.

“Tonight, then?” Gentry said.

“We’ll see,” I said.

CHAPTER 16

PHOEBE, RIDIN' SIDESADDLE, looked a muddy mess. But she was handlin' it well.

"How old a man is Wayne?" she asked.

"I don't rightly know."

"If you had to guess."

We were on safe but uneven terrain, pickin' our way through scrub pine with no trail in sight. Visibility was sparse, and would be for the next three or four miles. What open areas we found were heavy with bushes. Our horses were fidgety, havin' picked up the scent of bear, cougar, or wolves. I was more concerned about wolves, havin' heard a pack howlin' a couple hours before Ira Glass tried to kill me. Their cries had started miles away and grew fainter durin' the night, suggestin' they were movin' away from us.

But they could always turn around.

I stood in my stirrups and made a wide sweep with my eyes, searchin' for any motion in the bushes that shouldn't be there.

"Emmett?"

Phoebe again. She'd asked me somethin' personal about Shrug three times since the Indian attack.

"Shrug's age is hard to pin down," I said. "He could be anywhere from twenty to forty. Maybe older. Or younger."

"Emmett Love," she said, "I'm being serious."

"Me too," I said.

"Will he pay us a dinner visit before we reach Springfield?"

"It ain't likely."

"Why not?"

"Shrug don't like bein' around groups of people. He's not overly social."

"I find him charming."

I turned to look at her. "If you want, I can ask if he'd like to have dinner with you."

Phoebe's face was caked in mud, so I couldn't tell if she blushed. "It wouldn't be proper," she said.

"I guess not."

"Unless you'd care to join us," she added.

"I think I might already have plans," I said.

"With Gentry? She's a child!"

We rode in silence a minute. Then I said, "Gentry's mighty well-formed for a child."

"You should have the decency not to notice how well she's formed."

"That type of formation is mighty hard to overlook," I said.

"It should neither be noticed, nor commented on."

"Well, I believe you're the one brought it up."

"I most certainly did not. And beyond everything else, she's half your age."

"Maybe. But she don't seem to care."

"Well, go ahead and fornicate with her, then. See if I care."

We were quiet a few more minutes before I said, "Would you?"

"Would I what?"

"Care if I fornicate with Gentry?"

She started to speak, then paused. Finally she said, "Of course not. I'm practically a married woman. Why should I care what you do or to whom you do it?"

CHAPTER 17

IN WARMER MONTHS, the mosquitoes along the White River are the most determined you'll find this side of the Mississippi. So thick and fierce are they, I've heard stories of men and dogs bein' driven crazy while polin' the river from here to Yellville, Arkansas. Campin' along the banks of the White would've been impossible a month ago, but we were four days from October, and the biggest issue we faced was the frigid water. Phoebe had been standin' on the riverbank, watchin' the whores yelp and frolic in the water. But somethin' made her turn and walk back to where I was buildin' a fire.

"You're not jumpin' in?" I asked.

"In due course. Right now the others are having a—a contest."

"What sort of contest?"

"I'll not say the word. But it's the sort of contest you'd be pleased to judge."

I stood and turned my attention to the creek, wonderin' what she could possibly be talkin' about. Then it hit me: the whores were havin' a nipple contest.

"Sure you don't want to join in?" I said. "It ain't the overall size of the bosom, it's the length of the tips that count."

"Thank you, no," she said, her voice full of frost. "But it's obvious you're aware of the judging criteria."

"The what?"

"You've obviously done this before."

"Well, I've not been a contestant, if that's what you mean."

She closed her eyes, put her hands on each side of her head, and muttered somethin'. Then she went and pulled a bar of soap from her kit and started walkin' down river.

"Don't go too far," I said. "And be sure to finish your bath before it gets dark."

I pulled a fish hook out of my kit, tied some string to it, then went to the riverbank and turned wood over 'til I found some grub worms. I paused a minute to watch the women. Phoebe was right, I'd had some experience with cold water nipple contests among the whores I've brought out west. Funny thing, the winners are never the big-jugged gals like Scarlett. It's always one of the skinny ones you'd never expect. In this group the clear winner was Leah. But had I been judgin' on overall appearance, and if Monique was to be excluded, I'd a' picked Gentry.

I tipped my hat to her, and got a kiss blown back in return.

Headin' up river fifty yards, I found a quiet pool that had a huge dead tree lyin' in it. I stepped onto the tree trunk and walked about fifteen feet and sat down. It took about five minutes to land the first perch, and I quickly landed three more. But the next quarter hour went by without a nibble. By then, dusk was settin' in, so I hopped in the river to clean the caked mud off me, then packed up the perch and headed back to camp.

The women were sittin' on rocks around the fire, naked under their blankets. Gentry winked and blew me a kiss as I passed by. Scarlett stood to meet me and held out her hand.

"I'll clean 'em for you, Emmett," she said.

I handed her the perch.

"Thanks, Scarlett. If you start these, I ought to have some more by the time you're done." I looked around. "Anyone seen Phoebe?"

They hadn't.

I was a little surprised, but not concerned. It wouldn't be dark for another half hour or more, and Phoebe had gotten a late start. Also, proper women take twice as long to wash their clothes as whores, 'cause whores will strip naked and wash everythin' at once. Proper women remove their clothes one piece at a time to wash 'em. I figured to give her another fifteen or twenty minutes, and if she weren't back by then, I'd take one of the women with me to fetch her. I'd do it myself, 'cept I wouldn't want her to think I was spyin' on her.

"Emmett?" Gentry said. "Can I fish with you?"

A couple of the women snickered.

"I reckon you can," I said.

Gentry's face lit up and she scrambled to her feet and raced to my side.

Monique rolled her eyes and declared, "*Elle baiserait une pile de roches en souhaitant un serpent.*"

"Don't wait up for us," Gentry said, laughin'.

"Measure him close," Emma said. "We've got money on how big he gets."

"Oh, Lord," I said.

"If he wears you out, give me a shout!" Leah hollered.

As Gentry and I passed the point where we could be seen, I heard Scarlett sigh, "Guess we'll have to make do with four perch for dinner. Anyone got some corn dodgers?"

CHAPTER 18

I HAD EVERY intention of puttin' my line in the water and provin' Scarlett wrong, but once we sat down on the riverbank Gentry was on me like sparkle on gold dust. She coaxed sounds out of me I would a' laughed to hear come from another man. While it ain't no secret whores know how to pleasure a man, in my experience them that love doin' it are few and far between. If Gentry didn't love what she was doin', she sure had me fooled, 'cause she was the best I ever had. So skilled was she at ruttin', I may have said I loved her! I may have said it twice, even though the whole episode took less than five minutes. Durin' the time I said it, I *did* love her. If I thought for one minute she'd continue to service me like that into old age, I'd a' promised to make an honest woman of her right then and there. But passion don't stay put in a younger woman's heart, and it would only be a matter of time before she'd want to rut a man her own age. And when that time came, she'd do so, whether I loved her or not.

"Scarlett said you were a screamer," I said.

"Did she?"

"But you never screamed tonight."

Gentry placed her palm on my cheek and kissed my lips. "I didn't need to scream tonight, Emmett."

"Why? Was I that bad?"

"A' course not!"

"Then why?"

"I didn't scream because I love you."

"That don't make sense."

"I didn't have to pretend tonight, Emmett."

"You sayin' you enjoyed it?"

"A' course I did!"

I stroked her hair.

"Emmett?"

"Yeah?"

"Why did you ask me that?"

"Well, we were both doin' it, but I was the only one makin' all the noises."

"So?"

"I'm not sure I did my best."

"Oh, Emmett," she said. "It's not *how* you do it that counts."

"It ain't?"

"Hell's bells, Emmett! *Anyone* can fuck. It's what's between us that makes our fuckin' special."

We were quiet a minute. Then I said, "Still, I like to feel I did my best. And this went awful quick."

She giggled. “I suppose it did.” Then she said, “You wanna try again?”

“I do indeed.”

She pulled me onto her and said, “Then, come and get it, cowboy!”

And I would’ve, except that somewhere down river, Phoebe started screamin’ fit to bust.

CHAPTER 19

"GO BACK TO camp and tell the women to get their guns out!" I said.

"Don't go off and get yourself killed, Emmett," Gentry said.

I pulled up my pants and strapped on my holster.

"Run!" I said. "And shoot anyone who tries to enter camp."

"What if it's you comin' back? Or Phoebe?"

"We'll shout our names before comin' in."

I took off runnin' down the riverbank, thankful I'd kept my boots on when ruttin' with Gentry. It was dark enough to force me to watch my feet, but barely light enough to see 'em.

After two minutes I stopped to listen.

Everything was quiet.

I felt terrible.

I'd teased Phoebe into an argument and allowed her to stomp away on her own, somethin' I'd a' never done had we made camp in a more dangerous place. But what was I thinkin'? There *are* no safe places. Just 'cause we'd never had trouble in this neck of the woods don't mean there couldn't *be* trouble.

I took a few steps while fightin' the urge to shout her name. If a critter had her, and she was alive, she'd still be screamin'. If travelers or Indians had her, they'd a' raped or killed or run off with her, and if she was conscious, she'd be screamin'. But she weren't screamin', which meant she was likely dead or unconscious.

I ran a couple more minutes, 'til I figured to be very close to where Phoebe had been when she screamed. I stopped again to listen, but heard nothin'. I realized now how trouble had found us. The whores had been hollerin' when playin' in the river, and sound carries a long way over open water. Someone or some type of critter could a' heard 'em up to two miles away. Hell, Shrug could a' heard 'em from *three*. Which meant Shrug probably heard Phoebe's scream too, from wherever he'd been. Unless he thought it was part of the whores playin'.

In the back of my mind I realized I'd relied on Shrug far too much, assumin' he's always near, watchin' over us. Sometimes he's way out in front of us, or makin' a wide circle around us, dependin' on where he thinks the danger is. Earlier today, he hadn't known about the Indians, and I'd expected him to pop up next to me on the riverbank when I'd been fishin'. It would a' been just like Shrug to be standin' there with a string of perch, all bigger than mine, pointin' and grinnin' at my string. Shrug would've expected to eat fish tonight, and might've even come into camp to get some. But he hadn't so much as whistled or laid a stone since shortly after the Indian attack.

It suddenly crossed my mind that Shrug could a' been injured by the Indians before they attacked me. They were poor with rifles, but deadly with bows and arrows. When the shootin' started, Shrug probably heard it and worked his way back to the mountain. He may have killed the Indians I didn't shoot.

I wondered if he'd been hit by an arrow. I didn't see any blood by the stones he'd placed after the battle, which was a good sign. But I couldn't be certain Shrug wasn't hurt. If he had been, he could still be up on that mountain, tendin' to his wounds.

And I'd left him there.

And never thought a second thought about it.

But whether that's what happened to Shrug, or whether somethin' else happened, there was no escapin' the fact that I'd been careless, and now poor Phoebe was payin' the price.

I started walkin' slowly down river, tryin' to put all thoughts of Shrug out of my mind. If he was hurt, I'd deal with it later. If he was nearby, so much the better. Suddenly, I heard Phoebe make three quick, muffled noises close by. It almost sounded like she was tryin' to call out, but couldn't, like maybe someone had his hand over her mouth.

Which told me she wasn't mortally hurt.

If she had been, I'd be able to hear her pain sounds.

Whatever had befallen her, at least she was alive.

Which meant I could still save her.

I slid my Colt out of the holster and felt the tip of the barrel to make sure no twigs or mud had got in it, then silently put it back in place. I pulled some bullets out of my gun belt and stuffed them in my left pocket, so I could reload quickly if need be.

I crept slowly along the riverbank, careful not to snap any twigs. When I came to the edge of a thicket I knew I couldn't go any further without wakin' the dead. I slowly backtracked to the river, put my gun on the ground, and quietly stepped into the water 'til I reached a depth of five feet. I crouched down so that only my nose and head were above water, and then I moved slowly down river another fifty feet.

There on the riverbank, twenty-five feet away, I saw Shrug.

Fuckin' Phoebe.

Or maybe Phoebe was fuckin' Shrug.

From where I stood in the river, it was hard to tell who was fuckin' who. But they both seemed to be enjoyin' it.

I almost passed out from relief that Phoebe and Shrug were okay. Then I nearly passed out over the fact that Little Miss Proper was actually fuckin' someone she barely knew, right out in the open, on a riverbank!

The proper thing to do was turn my head and walk away, like when some young cowboy's had too much to drink and challenges me to a fight he can't win. But this weren't one a' them times where walkin' away would save someone's life. And it didn't make me feel bad to stay put. I reckon I should a' felt worse than I did about spyin' on 'em, but it was like watchin' a cyclone form in the clouds: it ain't what you expected to see, or what you *hoped* to see, but once it starts, you want to keep a close eye on it.

It weren't the kind of fuckin' you'd expect to see on a riverbank, where there's all sorts of creepy, crawly things slitherin' about at night. Hell, the chiggers and ticks *alone* would make me want to keep my drawers mostly on. I'd a' thought others felt the same way, and would keep as much clothin' on as possible, when riverbank fuckin'.

But not these two.

They were buck naked.

It was dark, but not so dark I couldn't see Phoebe's milky thighs straddlin' Shrug's broken body. She arched her back and moved her hips and tossed her head back and began moanin' softly. She cupped her breasts in her hands and—well, at that point I knew I'd intruded enough.

Good for Shrug, I thought, and slowly waded back to where I'd left my gun.

CHAPTER 20

"EVERYTHIN'S FINE," I called out to the women from a distance. "You can put your guns down."

Gentry said, "Thank God you're okay!"

"Where's Phoebe?" Scarlett said.

"She'll be along directly."

I entered the camp and took a spot by the fire.

"Is she okay?" Scarlett said.

"She's fine."

"You spoke to her?" Hester said.

"No."

"But she screamed," Gentry said. "I heard her. Three or four times."

"She screamed 'cause the water was cold."

"You watched her bathe?" Gentry said.

"I didn't spy on her," I said. "Only got close enough to see she was okay, then came back. But don't talk to her about it."

"Why not?" Mary asked.

"I don't want her to think I was peepin'."

"Did you see her naked?" Gentry asked.

"Nope."

"You sure?"

"Positive. She was deep in the river while I was there."

"Good."

"You save me any fish?" I asked.

Scarlett laughed. "There ain't enough fish in the whole damn river for the appetite you worked up tonight. But we saved you a share."

I looked at Gentry's face in the firelight. "You told 'em?"

"There was no use denyin' it," she said.

"In case you care, I won the bet," Mary said.

"Shut up, Mary!" Gentry snapped. To me, she said, "I'm sorry, Emmett. I was proud, is all."

"No harm done," I said. "So, what was the winnin' number?"

"Seven fingers," Mary said.

I frowned. "That don't seem like a lot."

Mary laughed. "It ain't."

"Who guessed the highest?" I said.

"Gentry guessed ten," Scarlett said, laughin'.

"Wait. There are seven of you. You mean someone picked four?"

"Emma only used her left hand," Mary said.

The women guffawed and spent the next twenty minutes talkin' about how many fingers their biggest customers measured. All their stories started well above ten, though Gentry was kind enough not to speak of her experiences in front of me.

"I'm coming into camp," Phoebe called out.

"We were worried about you," I said.

"I'm sorry. I enjoyed the water so much I lost all track of time, and it turned dark before I knew it. I had to pick my way back carefully, so I wouldn't turn an ankle or tear my clothes."

"Well, we saved you some fish," I said, though I was sure Shrug had fed her.

"Oh, I'm not hungry," she said. "Please, divide my share and enjoy it."

"You seem happier comin' back than when you left," Hester said.

"It's good to be clean, and this close to Springfield," Phoebe said.

"Well, it suits you," Scarlett said. "This is the most I've heard you talk the whole trip."

Mary said, "While you were gone, Gentry fucked Emmett."

"Why, thank you for sharing that with me, Mary," Phoebe said.

CHAPTER 21

WE TROTTED INTO Springfield around 9:30 the next mornin', and went straight to the little ranch where Rose kept the oxen and wagons. Though only twenty, Rose owns the ranch and ten acres that surrounds it. She also owns houses in Wichita, St. Louis, Denver, Seattle, and San Francisco. Claims she inherited 'em when her various husbands passed on. I don't know how much to believe about Rose, but I put nothin' past her.

"I've set the table for ten," Rose said, as we approached.

"How'd you know there was nine of us?" Leah said.

Rose studied her a moment. "You won the titty contest?"

Leah nearly fell off her horse.

Scarlett crossed herself and said, "Don't even *look* my way!"

Monique, seein' the fear in Scarlett's eyes, crossed herself too.

Phoebe leaned toward me. "How does she know these things?"

Rose turned to Phoebe, and smiled. "I bet *you* slept well last night!" she said.

Phoebe blushed, and I forced myself not to smile. All mornin' I'd been wonderin' what would cause a woman like Phoebe to fornicate with Shrug. Was it because he'd saved her life and she felt grateful? Was it because they'd forged a close bond with their conversations? Was it curiosity? Pity? Was it somethin' sacred, or just a last fling before gettin' married? The whole thing didn't make sense to me. Then again, I never was very good at cipherin' women's reasons for the things they do.

"And you, Emmett," Rose said.

"What?"

"How did *you* sleep last night?"

"It were a long trip," I said. "We *all* slept well last night."

She looked at Gentry. "Some better than others, I suspect."

"You're scarin' me," Gentry said. Then added, "No offense."

Monique shrieked, "*Mon Dieu!*"

She was pointing at Rose's cat.

"That's Rugby," Rose said.

"Jesse's ballocks!" Gentry cursed. "Where's his fur?"

"He's a hairless cat."

"On purpose?"

Rose looked at me and said, "I see why you're fond of her."

"Does he bite?" Mary asked.

"Like a banshee," Rose said. "But he won't be joining us on the trip, so you needn't worry."

Rugby jumped into Rose's arms, and from there hopped onto her shoulder, where he perched like a parrot.

"This is my tenth Rugby," Rose said.

"What happened to the other nine?" Mary said.

"They died after living to a ripe old age."

"How is that possible?" Phoebe said.

"I'm an old soul," Rose said. "But enough about me. Climb off your horses and join me for breakfast."

Phoebe whispered, "Is it safe, Emmett?"

"It'll be the best breakfast you ever ate," I whispered back.

Rose's ranch hand, Roberto, appeared, and offered to take our horses to the corral. We let him. Then we entered Rose's kitchen.

"Look at the size of that table!" Hester said.

As the women washed for breakfast, I helped put the platters of food on the table. There was corn bread, biscuits with currant jelly, boiled eggs, hot cakes, sausages, fried potatoes, salt beef hash with onions, and some other stuff I'd never seen.

Phoebe leaned over one such platter.

"How on earth did you come by scrapple?" she said.

"What's scrapple?" I said.

"Smell it," Phoebe said.

I did.

"Heavenly, isn't it?"

It was. We looked at Rose.

"It's common food in Philadelphia," Rose said, simply.

Phoebe said, "Were you aware I'm from Philadelphia?"

"No, but I've spent time there."

We each found something special. For me it was apple sauce, which I hadn't had since I was a kid. Monique had a plate of fresh lemon tarts. Scarlett found peaches. Emma said, "Oh, my God! Oyster pie!"

And so it went.

As we ate, Rose said, "The women left without us."

She was referrin' to the Springfield whores we planned to take to Dodge City.

"All five?" I said.

Rose nodded. "They left on Wednesday."

I paused. I had a history with one of 'em, and was surprised to hear she hadn't waited for me.

"Gina went with 'em?" I said.

Gentry raised an eyebrow at me, but said nothin'.

"Sorry, Emmett," Rose said. "Some dandy came through town, said he'd relocate them in Wichita."

"Someone you know?"

"No, and I don't think he knows what he's doing."

"Why'd they go?"

She shrugged. "Guess they trusted him."

Gentry stared at me, as if wonderin' how upset I might be about Gina not comin' with us. When I said, "Well, that knocks the profit outta the trip," it seemed to ease Gentry's mind.

Rose shrugged. "Something will turn up."

"I hope to hell so," I said.

After breakfast, Rose said, "Emmett, there's a bucket of water on the back porch you can use to clean the dishes. Gentry, come with me."

Gentry looked at me before moving.

"It's okay," I said. "You can trust Rose."

They left the kitchen together and didn't come back 'til we finished the dishes. When they walked in, Mary saw Gentry's face and started snickerin'.

"Don't you *dare* laugh!" Gentry said, makin' a fist. She had some sort of yellow cream all over her face and neck.

"What's that?" I said.

"A poultice," Rose said. "In two days Gentry will be the prettiest girl in the county. Next to me, of course."

It was true that Rose was beautiful. She had thick black hair and milk-white skin the sun couldn't darken, even the slightest shade. Her eyes were big and green, and her brows angled sharply above 'em, as if shaped by a sculptor. She was slight, but sturdy, with a useful swell in her chest, and long legs. Her hips were narrow, and better for starin' at than birthin' babies.

I'd originally planned to spend the afternoon buyin' supplies for the trip, and roundin' up the town whores and gettin' their stuff packed on the wagons so we could leave the next mornin'. But there weren't no Springfield whores to take, and Rose already had the supplies we'd need, so we loaded two wagons instead of three, hitched the oxen to 'em, and began our western journey a day early.

Since Rose's oxen were better suited for pullin' wagons, she paid the whores a fair price for their horses and mule, and kept 'em in her corral, where Roberto could tend to 'em. Scarlett drove the whores in one wagon, and Rose and Phoebe drove the supply wagon. Major and I led the way.

Because the Kansas draught had turned normal people desperate and deadly, I decided to take the old hunter-trapper trails, instead of the main ones. The problem with that plan was there'd be no water 'til Cherryville, some hundred and twenty miles from the Missouri border. If the draught was still goin' strong, the water Shrug and I knew about in Cherryville might be dried up as well. If that turned out to be the case, we wouldn't be able to fill the barrels 'til we got to the Arkansas River, thirty miles west of Newton. Of course, Wichita was closer, and had plenty of water, bein' located right beside the Arkansas River. But I wanted to avoid goin' there 'cause demand for whores was so high, if the locals knew I had a wagon full of 'em, they'd likely kill me and force the women into service.

Plannin' for the worst, we loaded six large water barrels onto Rose's wagon, intendin' to fill 'em at Copper Lake, twenty miles outside the Kansas border.

"Do we need that many barrels for the trip?" Phoebe asked.

"No. Two for us, two for the livestock."

"And the other two?"

"I brought a couple of women to East Kansas a few months ago," I said. "If they're still where I dropped 'em off, and alive, they're gonna want some water by now."

"Why Emmett," she said. "That's quite noble of you."

I didn't know what to say, so I just said, "Thank you."

"Don't be modest," she said, "it's very gallant. You've caught me by surprise."

"How's that?"

"I wouldn't have expected such thoughtfulness."

"From a coward who can't shoot rabbits?"

She smiled. "Perhaps I was a bit hasty in my assessment of you."

"Perhaps you were," I said.

"Well then, I apologize."

I nodded. "Apology accepted."

"Your soul might be worth saving," she said.

"You think?"

"Every now and then a glimmer shines through."

"Well, maybe I'll bring you somethin' next time I come through Newton," I said.

"I doubt I'll be wanting for anything," Phoebe said, "but a visit would be most welcome, I'm sure."

"Then I'll look in on you sometime," I said, and meant it.

I worried for Phoebe's future.

I doubted the rancher she planned to marry had any cattle left, or grass to graze 'em. The great draught of 1856 had been bad, but this one was far worse. Problem with Kansas, there ain't no natural lakes. What water they have comes from rivers and rain barrels, and last I heard, the Kansas River had got so narrow, it could be forded at any point. I figured half the population of East Kansas would have moved away or thirsted to death by now.

CHAPTER 22

A COUPLE HOURS into the trip, I heard the whores callin' my name. It weren't a fearful call, more like a teasin' one. I sighed and backtracked a hundred yards to their wagon.

"What's wrong?" I said.

"Can I ride with you?" Gentry said.

"Wouldn't be right to make Major carry two, less it was an emergency."

"But I'm so bored!"

"We've got room for you in the wagon, Emmett," Scarlett said, which set all the girls to titterin'.

Gentry's yellow poultice face lit up. "Please Emmett?" she coaxed.

I hate wagon ridin'.

It's bumpy and slow and hurts my back and neck somethin' fierce.

But I didn't want Gentry to feel she'd given her considerable charms last night to an ingrate.

"Maybe I will," I said.

We stopped the wagon Scarlett was drivin', and I tied Major to the back of it and climbed in and sat beside Gentry. When I got settled, she kissed my cheek. It weren't a pleasurable kiss, due to the stench comin' off the poultice, which smelled like wet goat hair and rotten fish.

Mary said, "There ain't nothin' worse than a schoolgirl's crush on a cowboy."

By the time we traveled fifty feet I had to shift my position in the wagon twice, which prompted Mary to ask if I had somehow caught the crabs recently.

Gentry stiffened.

Before things came to blows, Scarlett said, "Anyone know a good joke?"

Hester said, "I do."

"Tell it then," I said.

"Ever hear about the whore house for women with no legs?"

"Nope," I said.

"You ought to check it out."

"Why's that?"

"I hear the place is *crawling* with pussy!"

"Oh Lord!" I said.

Emma fondled her breasts and said, "Let's play that question game with Emmett."

"Sounds like fun," I said, noticin' Gentry's eyes were still smolderin' over Mary's insult. "But don't start with me, since I never played before."

"We'll ask you last, then," Leah said.

I was grateful for the skillful way these women could change a subject so quickly. I guessed they probably had to develop that talent to keep cowboys from killin' each other when they come to town spoilin' for a fight.

My thoughts got interrupted when one of the wagon wheels hit a partic'larly large rock. I gritted my teeth and winced. Figured I'd bide my time an hour or so, then make up some excuse to get off this hell wagon.

The girls asked each other one crazy question after another, most of which involved fornication, and I was glad Phoebe was ridin' in the supply wagon with Rose, and couldn't hear 'em. Their answers seemed impossible, but no less believable than the stories I've heard Rose tell. When they got to me, Mary said, "Okay, Emmett. What's the most peculiar thing you ever saw?"

Everyone turned to me. Even Scarlett, who was busy drivin' the oxen.

"Well, I don't rightly know how to answer that," I said. "What I think is peculiar might not raise your eyebrow."

"C'mon, Emmett, Hester said. "I told you about the two-headed turkey and the dancin' bear."

"And a helluva story it was!" I said.

"Then tell us yours. What's the strangest but true thing you ever saw?"

"Well, don't know if it's the strangest, but it's true enough."

They waited for me to continue. I sighed and gave it up.

"Five years ago Jimmy Bass shit a live fish."

"What?" Emma said.

"Are you *serious*?" Leah said.

Gentry clapped her hands and squealed with laughter.

Scarlett's face was full of doubt.

"It's true," I said. "We were halfway across Kansas at the time, and there weren't a lake or river within fifty miles. Still, Jimmy squatted to shit and a fish came out."

"A *live* one?" Gentry said.

"Live as any fish you'd catch in a creek. Flappin' around in the dirt, jumpin' up five or six inches in the air and wigglin' about."

"And his name was Jimmy *Bass*?" Scarlett said.

"Coincidence, ain't it?" I said.

"Too much so," she said. She rolled her eyes and turned her attention back to the trail.

"You actually *saw* it come out?" Mary said.

"Well, I weren't watchin' him do his business, but when he screamed, I come runnin' and couldn't help but notice half a fish stickin' out his ass. He grunted and pushed, and then the fish hit the ground and started flip-floppin'."

The girls laughed 'til Emma said, "Which end of the fish came out first?"

"The tail."

"Was it wigglin'?"

I nodded. "Like a toddler in church."

Scarlett turned around again to face me.

"How big was it?" she said.

"About six inches. More or less."

"That's a common size for a lot of things that have to do with men," Leah said.

"Maybe he had it in his kit the whole time, and stuffed it in his butt before you saw him," Emma said.

"Well, he'd have had to carry that fish fifty miles in the heat," I said.

"Maybe he kept it in a wet rag and poured canteen water on it regular," Leah said.

"I don't believe you could keep a fish alive that way for fifty miles," I said. "Nor frisky, neither."

"Maybe he caught the fish fifty miles earlier and hid it in the water barrel," Gentry said.

The wagon went quiet.

We all looked at her.

"I'll be damned," I said.

Scarlett frowned. Probably disappointed in herself for not figurin' it out.

I frowned too.

"I'm sorry he tricked you, Emmett," Gentry said.

I said, "I'm surprised the water barrel never crossed my mind."

"Well, you were probably just taken by surprise," Gentry said.

"At the time, maybe. But I've had five years to ponder it, and still never figured it out."

Scarlett said, "What happened to the fish?"

"Jimmy ate it," I said.

CHAPTER 23

BEFORE LONG I was back on my horse, feelin' much more comfortable.

I hadn't seen any sign of Shrug since he fucked Phoebe on the riverbank, but I knew he was out there somewhere, keepin' an eye out. There was no reason for him to lay down stones, since there was but one destination we could be headin' for with all these water barrels, and Shrug would know what it was. I hoped to run into him at Copper Lake so I could ask him about Phoebe. I didn't know exactly *what* to ask, but I had to ask *somethin'*. But as I rode some more, I changed my mind. I decided not to say a word about it unless he brought it up.

Thinkin' about all this made me start day dreamin' about what I'd seen: Phoebe naked, her long hair loose and whippin' around like it had been caught in a cyclone, white hips pumpin' steady as a railroad engine with a full head of steam. I conjured up her image in my mind to the point I almost missed the stones that lay a mere ten feet in front of me.

I pulled Major to a halt and looked around.

The whole area was low-land prairie, meanin' there was nothin' to either side of us, and before us, nothin' but the rutted miner's trail. I stood in my stirrups and looked back the way we'd come.

Nothin' followin' us.

There were four stones, with no directional fifth one. For whatever reason, Shrug was tellin' me to stop.

But why?

I cursed.

Dependin' on how long he wanted us to wait, we might not make Copper Lake before dark. If that happened, we wouldn't be able to fill the water barrels 'til mornin'. I'd a whole lot rather fill 'em tonight, and get an early start tomorrow.

I had half a mind to keep movin', but Shrug ain't never been wrong before, so I waited 'til the wagons caught up to me. Then I said, "We're gonna sit tight awhile, and rest the livestock. Ladies, this'd be a good time to relieve yourselves, if you got the urge."

The women climbed out of the wagon and wandered around to get the blood flowin' in their legs. Some of 'em squatted in the prairie grass to piss. Rose hopped off her wagon and tied her reins around a large rock. Then she walked over to me and Major.

I said, "You have any idea why he wants us to stop here?"

She closed her eyes and tilted her head skyward.

I waited.

She moved her head slightly, from side to side, swayin' like she could hear some type of silent music.

I waited some more.

Finally, she said, "Someone's coming."

"Who, Shrug?"

"A wagon. Heading right for us." She pointed westward.

I stood in my stirrups again and stared a long time.

"There ain't nothin' there," I said.

"It's coming," she said.

I'd never known Rose to be wrong before, but this time she had to be. The land to the west was flat and clear, far as the eye could see, which was at least five miles. If there was anythin' headin' our way, I'd a'seen it.

Rose pointed again.

"There it is," she said.

I frowned and followed her finger. No one's eyes were better than mine, and there was no wagon, nor anythin' else comin' from that direction. Not man, beast, nor bird.

And then there was.

Far off in the horizon, I was able to make out the wispy lines of somethin' that weren't there a few seconds earlier. It was so far away it could a'been anythin', but a half hour later I could see it was a covered wagon, pulled by two oxen. Another half hour passed, and the man and woman sittin' in the front waved at us.

"They'll be here in fifteen minutes," I said.

Rose said, "They're not alone."

"You mean there's more folks in the wagon?"

"There's a child. And something else."

"What, a dog? A cat?"

"No."

"Then what?" I said.

"Death."

CHAPTER 24

IT DIDN'T SEEM like no death wagon to me. In fact, the man and woman seemed right friendly, judgin' by how many times they waved at us while approachin'. Their wagon was weathered and gray, and covered with a dirt-colored canvas that had probably started out bein' white. The wheels hadn't been greased in awhile, causin' 'em to make an angry squeal with each turn. Someone had attached half-barrels of water on each side of the wagon, and I wondered how much water might be in 'em. When they got about ten minutes from us, their little girl joined them on the wagon seat. She looked to be eight or nine, and from this distance seemed to have very little expression on her face. She had blond hair and blue eyes and wore a gray dress that looked to be made of burlap, and a blue necklace that seemed too old for her.

The whores and Phoebe wanted to run and greet 'em, but I put a stop to that nonsense right quick. I told 'em to take up positions on and around the wagons and keep their rifles in their hands or on their laps.

"That's rude," Phoebe said.

"Maybe so," I said, "but it don't pay to be too friendly on the prairie. At least 'til you know who you're bein' friendly to."

The family pulled their wagon to a noisy stop about forty feet from us. Then the man, one of the biggest I'd ever seen, climbed down and started walkin' toward me.

I stayed on my horse.

"Howdy," he said, extendin' his hand.

"That's close enough," I said.

He stopped abruptly.

"Anythin' wrong?" he said. "It's just me and the missus, and our daughter."

I looked at the woman and child on the bench seat. The little girl stared straight ahead, like we weren't there. Though she showed no expression, her ma seemed right nervous.

"I don't shake hands," I said. "Nothin' personal."

"You a gunman?" he said.

"Nothin' personal," I repeated.

"That's quite all right," he said. He looked at the wagons and the women in 'em. "Whatcha got there?"

"A few folks headin' west."

Some of the ladies waved at the little girl. Instead of wavin' back, she stared straight ahead. I'd a' thought she'd be itchin' to run visit the women, but guessed she'd been told to stay put 'til her pa said it was okay.

"Looks like a bunch of women, dressed like men," the man said, wavin' at 'em. "And one of 'em's got a yaller face. She ain't diseased, is she?"

I looked him over. He wore the biggest cowboy hat I ever saw. Still, it seemed too small for his head. Maybe that was because he wore the brim high on his forehead, 'stead of low over his eyes, like most. He had on denim pants, which you don't see that often this side of the Rockies. He also had on purple boots, which you don't see anywhere.

"I'm Emmett Love," I said.

He smiled a big smile. "I'm Joe Simpson," he said. He pointed at the lady on the wagon seat and said, "And that there's my wife, Clara."

I tipped my hat without offerin' her a friendly expression.

"Ma'am," I said.

"Nice to meet you, Mr. Love," she said.

He pointed at the girl. "And this little bundle of happiness is Hannah."

She didn't appear to be filled with happiness, or even the least bit happy. But I nodded at her anyway, and she stared back at me with empty eyes in the way I've seen old men stare at a window without lookin' through it.

"Hannah would love to visit your womenfolk," Joe said, "if that suits you."

Hannah didn't look like she cared either way about visitin' with the women, but I didn't see no harm in it, other than the size of her pa. If he decided to turn surly, it could take several bullets to put him down.

I looked at Rose.

"What do you think?" I said.

Rose pulled her shotgun from the wagon and covered the distance to Joe Simpson so quick no one had time to react. She leveled her shotgun at the center of his face, pulled back the hammer on one of the chambers and said, "Hannah seems a bit solemn."

Joe laughed, not seemin' to realize the degree of danger his life was in.

"Hands in the air," Rose said.

He looked at me.

"I'd do it," I said.

Joe put his huge arms in the air.

"Hannah's just tired," he said. "Anyway, her bein' solemn don't seem enough reason to shoot a man."

"She's also got blond hair," Rose said.

He looked at his daughter.

"Can't deny it," he said.

"And you folks don't," Rose said.

"She come by her hair color honestly," he said. "Clara's family was all blonds."

They looked at each other a minute. Joe said, "Still ain't reason enough to shoot me over." Then he said, "Can I put my hands down now?"

Rose said, "You can put them down after I shoot you."

Joe shook his head. "You don't seem a neighborly bunch," he said. "But that's fine, we'll ask nothin' of you. If you'd see fit to lower your shotgun, Clara and I will be pleased to keep movin' along without troublin' you further."

Rose said nothin'.

"'Less you got more questions for me," Joe Simpson said.

"I do have one," Rose said.

"Please ask it, then."

Rose cocked the hammer on the second chamber of her shotgun. Then she said, "How did Hannah come by that necklace?"

CHAPTER 25

I HADN'T NOTICED Hannah's necklace bein' familiar 'til Rose asked the question.

Then it started to look real familiar. In fact, it looked a lot like the one my favorite whore from Springfield used to wear.

Clara spoke up. "Please don't shoot my husband!"

Rose inched the shotgun closer.

Joe said, "Whoa, Miss! Be careful with that thing!"

"The necklace," Rose said.

Clara's fingers raced to her daughter's throat. She pulled the necklace over Hannah's head and threw it on the ground in front of Rose. "Please! You can have it. It's just a cheap dry goods necklace," she said. "It's not valuable, and certainly not worth dying for."

Joe relaxed a bit. "I can explain the necklace," he said.

"Then do so," Rose said.

"It was a gift from a lady we met two days west of here," Joe said. "We found 'em ten miles off the main trail, five women and a man, travelin' together. Whores, I think, from Springfield, headin' to Dodge City. We made camp with 'em that night, and one of the whores, a pretty red-haired one, grew right fond of Hannah. She's the one give Hannah the necklace."

"It's true, Miss," Clara Simpson said. "Every word. I swear."

"Rose?" I said.

She didn't answer, nor take her eyes away from Joe Simpson.

I said, "It *does* sound like somethin' Gina might do, give her necklace to a cute little girl she'd grown attached to."

Ignorin' my comment, Rose said, "Tell your wife and daughter to climb down off the wagon."

Simpson sighed, and said, "Clara! Hannah! Do as she says."

They climbed down from the wagon and stood beside the ox team.

"Now walk over to us," Rose said.

From the water wagon, Phoebe shouted, "Rose, please. What's gotten into you?"

Rose ignored her.

"All three of you," she said. "Get on the ground, face down, with your hands behind your backs."

Joe gave me a questionin' look with his eyes. "Can't you do somethin'?" he said. "Your lady friend is scarin' my family. If it's our possessions you're after, you're welcome to 'em."

"I were you, I'd get on the ground, face down," I said.

"She wouldn't actually shoot us," Joe said. Then he said, "Would she?"

"Let me put it like this," I said. "She's twenty, and already buried six husbands."

The Simpson family hit the dirt like cow patties and put their hands behind their backs.

"Hold your gun on them, Emmett," Rose said.

I did.

Rose fetched the necklace from where it lay on the grass, examined it briefly, and tossed it to me.

"See those spots on it?" she said.

I did.

"That's blood."

"Blood?"

"From when he cut Gina's throat."

CHAPTER 26

"WELL, THE GIRL didn't cut no one's throat," I said.

Rose hollered, "Scarlett, come fetch Hannah. I doubt she's their kin, anyway."

Scarlett walked over and helped Hannah to her feet.

Rose said, "Get her comfortable, and find out what you can."

"You tell 'em nothin', girl, you hear?" the big man said. For the first time since we'd met him, his voice had menace in it.

"You got no call to question our girl," he said angrily.

"Shut up," Rose said.

Scarlett walked Hannah back to the whore wagon and picked her up and set her in it, and the whores instantly started makin' over her. Leah got her comb out and began running it through Hannah's hair. I believed what Rose said about Hannah not bein' kin to the Simpsons. If she was, she didn't seem concerned that her parents might get shot. Hell, she never said a word to 'em, nor even looked in their direction.

Rose made her way to the back of the Simpson's wagon, and climbed in. A few minutes later she came out with a disgusted look on her face.

"There are too many sizes of clothes to fit Clara," she said, "and too many possessions that don't match, including some books with other folks' names in them."

"All easily explained," Joe said, spittin' dirt from his lips.

"Save your breath," Rose said. "I can sniff a lie from twenty paces."

Five minutes passed, then Scarlett and Phoebe helped the child out of the wagon and took her to a small outcroppin' of rocks about fifty feet away. The three of 'em sat among the rocks, and spoke quietly.

"How long we gotta lay here in the dirt?" Joe Simpson said. "What you're doin' to us ain't right."

"We're thirsty," Clara said.

"Shut up," Rose said.

A half hour passed.

Then Scarlett called Rose over.

A few minutes later, Scarlett put Hannah back in the whore's wagon.

Rose walked over to me and nodded slowly.

I pointed at Clara.

Rose nodded again.

Then she fetched her reins and climbed in the supply wagon with Phoebe, and started headin' down the trail. Scarlett and the others followed in their wagon.

"What's goin' on?" Simpson said. "Where's everyone goin'?"

"Where's Hannah?" Clara said. "What did she tell them?"

"You ain't plannin' to take a kid's word for nothin', are you?" Joe Simpson shouted. "She's sick in the head! You can tell by lookin' at her she ain't right."

I didn't know what truths Hannah had revealed, but Phoebe wasn't makin' any kind of fuss, so whatever she said, it must a' been bad.

I didn't care for these Simpsons. They'd not only taken up the better part of my afternoon, they probably killed Gina and the rest of the group that left Springfield on Wednesday.

I felt like shootin' 'em right then and there.

But I didn't.

It wouldn't a 'been right.

Not to mention I'd a' felt terrible if the little girl heard me shoot 'em.

So I sat on my horse and guarded Joe and Clara Simpson while the wagons rolled north, toward Copper Lake. I offered 'em no water, nor did I speak a single word to 'em.

I sat there on my horse and waited a full hour before emptyin' my pistol in 'em.

CHAPTER 27

"WHAT HAPPENED TO the oxen?" Phoebe said, when I caught up to her and Rose.

"I cut 'em loose," I said. "Four oxen are hard enough to keep up with. We don't have the manpower to care for six."

"Will they survive?"

"They will."

"Where will they go?"

"They'll either follow us at a distance or head to Springfield, I reckon."

"How can you be so sure?"

"Oxen are pretty good about locatin' water," I said.

"What about the covered wagon?"

"I left it there. Why do you ask?"

"It might have constituted a fair dowry," Phoebe said.

"Dowry?"

"For Hiram."

"Who's Hiram?"

"Hiram Pickett."

"Who?"

"My betrothed."

"Your *what?*"

"My husband-to-be, you dolt."

"Well, I didn't think any thoughts about a dowry," I admitted.

"I'm just trying to be practical," she said. "It seems a waste to leave a perfectly good wagon on the prairie."

"I thought about bringin' it with us to sell," I said, "but I didn't want to upset the little girl."

"Her name is Hannah."

"Of course."

"Say it."

"Her name is Hannah," I said.

"You have no idea what she's been through," Phoebe said.

"Was she their daughter?"

"No."

"Then I don't want to know," I said.

I spurred my horse and galloped two hundred yards in front a' them and kept that distance between us 'til we made camp an hour south of Copper Lake.

While I rode, I thought about Rose, and how she sometimes gets feelin's about things and people that others don't. She calls it intuition, but whatever it is, it makes her a great travel companion. Also, she's uncommon good in the woods. She can find her way from one end to the other in pitch dark. I've seen her sniff out water, tubers, and medicinal roots, too. I doubt anyone's better in the woods than her. She claims it's because she grew up in a forest in Florida back in the pirate days, but that's just stories, like the ones she tells about all them husbands she claims to have married. Hell, the girl's only twenty. She couldn't a' known Gentleman Jack Hawley the pirate, or done all them things she claims. But I don't contradict her. If I did, she might stop tellin' her stories. And her campfire stories are the best I ever heard!

Rose is the finest nurse you could hope to have. Her knowledge of potions will match any big city doctor's. A year ago I caught a grazin' gun shot on my arm, outside a bar in Springfield. It weren't enough of a wound to barely hurt, so I thought little of it. Just poured some whiskey on it and went to bed. By the next night it was all swollen and oozy and hurt like the dickens. I'd seen cowboys die from wounds that looked like that, and never understood how such a little scratch could do so much damage. I got worried enough to go see Doc Inman. He took one look at my arm and said, "I ain't gonna lie to you, it's bad."

"Am I gonna die?" I said.

"You would have died," he said, "but I can fix this."

"How?"

"We'll have to take that arm off."

"You mean cut it off?"

"I'm sorry," he said.

"Will it hurt?"

"It will."

"Should I get drunk first?"

He laughed. "There ain't enough whiskey in Springfield to keep it from hurtin', but if you get drunk enough to pass out, that'll probably help. But I'll need to strap you to my table before I start cuttin'."

Well, I was right upset about it, and figured if this was my last night to hold a drink in my right hand, I'd rather drink the best liquor in the state, and that type of spirits was located at Rose's ranch. I showed up there and told her my story, and she shook her head.

"Let me see that arm," she said.

She took one look at it and said, "It's badly infected, and getting worse by the minute."

"Am I gonna die?" I said.

"You would have died," she said, "but I can fix this."

"You got a good saw?"

"I don't cut people's arms off, Emmett."

She boiled some kind of birch bark in water and poked it awhile 'til the water turned brown. Then she made me drink it.

"Damn, that tastes awful!" I shouted.

"Would you rather have Doc Inman cut your arm off?"

I sniffed the water.

"I believe I might," I said, but I was kiddin'.

I drank the potion and immediately got the trots.

She gave me more potion and I wound up with what Rose called an upset stomach. A better description is that she gave me the drizzlin' shits.

That night was rough, but two days later I felt like a new man. I couldn't wait to try out my new arm, so I went to see Doc Inman. I lifted him off the ground with the same arm he was gonna cut off. Then I used it to drag him out to the water trough, and tossed him in it. When he come up, gaspin' for air, I dunked him under again. I woulda done it again, and told him why, but then I remembered how Rose made me promise not to give her credit for fixin' my arm.

"Why not?" I said.

"I don't want the town folk to think I'm a witch," she said.

"You get that a lot?"

"I used to. And it wasn't much fun."

I promised her I wouldn't tell anyone about her doctorin', so I left that saw bones in the water trough and headed to the bar to test my hand at holdin' a shot glass.

Before you know it, Rose had me drinkin' a cup of that brown water potion every time we took a trip. She said it would prevent my next infection *before* I get shot.

"How do you know I'm gonna get shot?" I say.

She doesn't answer, just kisses my cheek and gives me a sad smile.

I don't like the taste of that birch water, but it don't give me the shits anymore, so that's a plus.

So Rose is a great nurse. And, like I said before, she's mighty good to look at. But good as she is at everythin' else, the best thing about travelin' with Rose is her cookin'.

An hour into sundown that night, she'd made molasses corn bread and chuck wagon stew, and biscuits with scrapple gravy. She pan fried thin slices of pig fat in the gravy drippin's, and it tasted good enough to make a jackrabbit slap a hound dog!

That night, we had two fires goin', about twenty feet apart. Phoebe, Rose and me were at one, and the rest of 'em were gathered around the other. We removed most of our valuables from the wagons, and placed them among us in piles.

We made a box camp, meanin' the two wagons were opposite each other, with our livestock on either side, formin' a border for us and our fires. This type of setup helps to keep stray animals from wanderin' into camp. The downside is, Indians have an easy time stealin' from the wagons, which is why we unloaded our valuables in the first place.

For awhile, Phoebe, Rose, and me didn't talk much, content to listen to pieces of conversation passin' between the whores and Hannah. Hannah still wasn't smilin', but we were pleased to see she'd begun talkin' some, even though her comments weren't optimistic yet. She never asked what happened to Joe and Clara, and best I could tell, seemed not to care.

Every now and then Gentry looked over at me and we'd share a smile. After one such smile Rose said, "She makes you happy."

"She does."

"Just then when you smiled at her, you looked like you were thinking of something funny, but sad. Is it her poultice?

"In a way," I said.

"Well, don't worry about that, because her face is going to be stunning by Monday morning. You believe me, don't you, Emmett?"

"I do."

"Making Gentry beautiful is a gift I'm giving you."

"I've never had a problem with her complexion," I said.

"I know you haven't."

"Then how is it a gift?"

"You'll see."

"When?"

"When she's beautiful, and still wants you."

Phoebe said, "Would you like me to leave so you two can talk?"

"'Course not," I said.

"I wouldn't want to intrude on your private thoughts," she said.

"They're not partic'larly meant to be private."

Rose said, "What made you sad a moment ago, Emmett?"

"This time next week we'll be in Dodge City," I said, "and I'll have to leave her there to face a hard life. She'll be fine and all with Mama Priss, 'specially after the poultice does its job. But I'm gonna miss her somethin' terrible."

"You will?"

"'Specially nights like this, when I'm sittin' by a fire, all alone."

"You'll think about this trip, and your thoughts will turn to Gentry. And you'll wonder how she's doing," Rose said.

"I will for a fact."

Phoebe said, "You've surprised me again, Emmett."

"How's that?"

"I hadn't realized your feelings for Gentry were so sincere."

"Well, they are," I said. "My feelin's for her run deep."

She nodded slowly, then said, "I'm glad to hear that."

To Rose, she said, "There is a certain redeeming quality flitting about him that's hard to pin down. But every now and then it shines through."

"Well, thank you," I said.

We sat quietly a moment, and then Phoebe said, "You told us what was sad about Gentry's smile. What was the funny part?"

I chuckled.

"Please," she said. "Tell me."

"I would, but I don't want to make you mad."

"I promise I won't get angry. Now please, tell me."

"Well," I said, "Gentry's sittin' there by the fire, and her poultice is meltin'."

"Go on," Phoebe said.

"And I was lookin' at it from a distance, and when she turns to the side, one cheek sort of looks like a stallion's pecker."

Phoebe jumped to her feet and shouted, "For the love of God!"

Then she stomped off to join the others.

Rose shook her head and said, "Really, Emmett."

I said, "I think Phoebe just broke her promise."

CHAPTER 28

"IT'S ABOUT THAT time," I said.

"Please, Emmett," Gentry murmured. "Just a few more minutes?"

We were a quarter mile from camp, on my blanket, on trampled grass at the top of a steep hill. Dawn was breakin', and the smell of Phoebe's coffee had caught up to us. I'd grown rather fond of her sissy coffee of late, and that was just one of the things I was gonna miss about her when we got to Newton. Her odd way of payin' a compliment and then gettin' furious with me was another.

"It's nearly daybreak," I said, "and we ain't had breakfast. Then it's an hour to Copper Lake, and when we get there, we've got six barrels to fill."

Gentry let out a yawn. "Can we just lie here a few minutes and talk?"

I didn't want to lie there and talk. The stink on her face made me want to gag. It was so vile I doubted my horse would take an apple from her mouth. I wondered how Gentry could stand it. She couldn't have grown used to it. If it were me, I'd rather be pimply.

"Can we, Emmett?"

"Well, we spoke some last night," I said.

"Last night was more about ruttin' than talkin'," she said.

"Well, it was good ruttin'."

"It was," she agreed. "But sometimes a girl needs more from a man than an eager ruttin' partner."

"That makes sense."

"So can we talk? Just a few minutes?"

"Okay. But just a few minutes."

"Will you hold me first?"

I put my arm under her head and winced, thinkin' about her poulticed face bein' up against my chest. At first, due to the smell, I hadn't wanted to. But the way she settled into me, the top of her head was between my nose and her face, so the stink weren't half as bad. I was so happy about it, I kissed her hair.

"That was sweet of you, Emmett," she said.

"What would you like to talk about?" I said.

"Well, is there anything you'd like to ask me? Anything at all?"

I thought about it a minute.

"There is one thing," I said.

"Good! That's a start!"

"It's somethin' I've been wonderin' awhile."

"Well, ask it then," she said.

"Okay. What I was wonderin' is, when you're ruttin' with cowboys and miners and such, what thoughts do you have?"

"*What?*"

"I was just wonderin' what you think about while you're bein' fucked by all them men."

Gentry started to speak, then didn't. After awhile she sighed, and said, "Well, I mostly just think about the two dollars I usually get to keep, and what it'll buy. I sometimes wonder how much longer it'll take him to finish, and I'm usually hopin' he don't hurt me when it's over. I worry about the drunks and bullies and angry ones, and I wonder about those who are kind to me."

"You do? What do you wonder about them fellers?"

"Some of the married men are surprisingly kind to me, and I sometimes wonder about their wives and children. I see them walkin' to and from church together, headin' to the hotel restaurant for a nice meal. I always wondered what it would be like to go for a stroll on a man's arm."

"You never strolled through town with a man?"

"Whores don't stroll, Emmett. But I used to daydream about havin' a fella that would be happy to take me for a stroll without expectin' anything in return."

"Like the married men in Rolla?"

"I sometimes wonder if they're walkin' with their wives through town, thinkin' about me. I know a lot of them rut their wives, thinkin' about me, 'cause they've said so."

"Don't make it true," I said.

"No, it don't," she said. "But I think it's true."

We were quiet a moment.

"It's probably true," I said. Then added, "Do you ever worry that the money they're payin' you is takin' food off their table, or medicine that could help their kids?"

"No."

She answered so quick I figured she was through talkin' on the subject. Below us, at the base of the hill, Rose had started fryin' up a pan of bacon, which meant there'd be biscuits directly. Rose had a way of fryin' biscuits in bacon grease that couldn't be copied. Her bacon, mixed with the scent of Phoebe's coffee, set my stomach to growlin'. But Gentry seemed not to care about breakfast. Lookin' for subjects to talk about, I said, "Hannah seems to be openin' up some."

"Poor child's been through a lot," Gentry said. "Even by *our* standards."

"She don't seem to like me much," I said.

"Why, Emmett! That ain't so!"

"She shies away from me, and won't look me in the eye."

"Well, that's only natural."

"Why?"

"You're a man."

"So?"

"Hannah's had a rough go with men. She's cautious, is all. 'Cause she don't know you yet. But she knows you're a good man."

"How does she know that?"

"We've all told her so!"

"Mary told her that?"

Gentry laughed. "Well, no, not Mary. But Mary don't like no one."

I'd pretty much run out of conversation. I could smell the biscuits on the fire, and wondered if they'd saved us any bacon. If we got up right then, we could have food on our plate in less than three minutes. I had to think of a way to get Gentry movin' without actin' like I didn't want to cozy up to her.

Then it hit me.

"Rose will probably want to change your poultice after breakfast, won't she?"

Gentry sighed. "I'll put you out of your misery, Emmett."

"What?"

"I know you're hungry. But can I ask you something before we head down the hill?"

"Sure."

"Do you ever get tired of trail ridin'?"

"Well, it gives me a place to go, and puts money in my pocket."

"True, but it's dirty and dangerous, and the weather's often terrible. And you pretty much spend the money you make by the time you're done, don't you?"

"Pretty much."

"Have you never thought of settlin' down someplace? You could be a sheriff or keep watch in a saloon or whorehouse."

Gentry had hit the nail on the head. I'd been thinkin' long and hard about that very subject for quite some time, though it would involve an ownership position, 'stead of workin' for someone else. Funny thing, if I decided to go through with it, I'd be settlin' in Dodge City myself. What I had was more of an opportunity than a plan. But it required a bit more thought, and I could see no benefit in bringin' it up this close to breakfast.

"I've done law work before," I said.

"Did you enjoy it?"

"Some parts of it."

"Like what?"

"Well, if you have to kill a man, at least you don't have to answer to the sheriff."

"Maybe you could find sheriff work someplace, get married, and have some kids. Would that sort of life suit you?"

I laughed. "I doubt there's many women linin' up for the privilege of marryin' the likes of me!"

"Well, if such a line starts to form, I'll take a spot right up front," she said.

"Well, that's a fine thing to say, Gentry."

"It's true, Emmett."

"I'm honored you feel that way," I said.

We lay there a minute, smellin' the coffee, bacon and biscuits.

"Will you think about me after you leave Dodge?" she said.

"Of course I will."

"You promise?"

"I'll think about you all the time."

"I'll think about you all the time, too."

"I'd like that," I said.

"And will you come see me when you pass through?"

"If I got the cash I will."

"I wouldn't charge you," she said.

"I'd like that even better," I said.

We probably would a' laid there like that a few more minutes, but the sudden sound of Monique gettin' murdered made us jump to our feet.

"Stay here!" I shouted.

Then I grabbed my rifle and went tearin' down the hill.

CHAPTER 29

JUMPIN' UP AND runnin' downhill like that will suck the breath out of you, and make your heartbeat pound in your ears. Within seconds I had a pain in my side that made me gasp for air. The terrain was grassy, and thank God there weren't much dew, 'cause if there had been, I'd a' tumbled ass over ears all the way to the bottom, and broke my leg in the process.

The trip down seemed to take forever. Although the grass was mostly dry, the ground beneath it was uneven, and littered with enough hidden rocks and prairie holes to be treacherous. I moved as fast as I could, hopin' not to twist an ankle.

As I got close to the camp I heard Rose shoutin' at everyone to be quiet.

A minute ago, lyin' beside Gentry, I assumed it was Monique that was bein' murdered, 'cause she'd hollered like a poisoned pig. But when I finally burst into the camp, my chest heavin' and poundin', I realized Monique wasn't bein' murdered at all.

Scarlett was.

CHAPTER 30

THE FIRST THING I saw was somethin' you don't see too often in this part of the country. And when you *do* see one, it don't look like this.

A Texas Longhorn bull was pawin' at the dirt on the wagon-rut trail just beyond camp, head lowered, ready to attack. Rose was approachin' him slowly, tryin' to talk him down. The whores were huddled up in the bed of the supply wagon, eyes fixed on Rose and the bull. Some covered their mouths with their hands, as if tryin' not to cry out. Leah and Monique were clingin' to each other like it was the end of days. Monique seemed grief-stricken, and Leah was tryin' to console her, while bein' as quiet as possible, so as not to spook the bull.

Phoebe saw me enter the camp.

I noticed the muddy mixture of dust and tears coverin' her face. Our eyes met. She didn't appear to be in shock, but she was displayin' lots of emotions at the same time. She was horrified, of course, and frightened. And probably glad to see me.

But there was somethin' more.

Phoebe had taken up a defiant stance on the driver's bench. Her body was coiled like a rattler ready to strike. She was on the verge of jumpin' out of the wagon to help Rose. In that moment, for the first time since layin' eyes on her, I saw Phoebe in a new light. She'd come a long way in a short time, as women will when they must, and that vision of her crouched on the edge of the wagon, ready to take on a wild bull if need be, is a sight I'll never forget.

But there was also a heavy sadness in Phoebe's face, and when she jutted her chin toward a heap of clothes a few feet to the right of the bull, I saw why.

It was Scarlett's body.

Lyin' face down on the ground.

I felt terrible about Scarlett, but I didn't want Phoebe to jump in the fray. I motioned her to back up. Then, keepin' an eye on Rose and the bull, I strode quietly but steadily to the wagon. The others saw me and everyone started whisperin' at the same time, and pointin' to Scarlett. I put my finger over my lips, signalin' them to quiet down. When they did, I whispered, "Where's Hannah?"

"We don't know," Hester whispered back.

"Scarlett took her to do her necessaries," Emma said. "Then we heard a thud, and saw the bull goring Scarlett."

I looked around. There weren't much cover, but there was some. Hannah was likely hidin' behind the low bushes twenty yards to the right of Scarlett's body. Knowin' Scarlett, she probably drew the bull's attention away from Hannah to protect her. That's just the type of woman she was. If she was dead, I'd miss her terribly. On the other hand, I knew Scarlett to be a tough, capable woman. I wondered if she might be playin' possum.

I looked at the mound of clothes.

"Has she moved or made a sound?" I whispered.

The women shook their heads.

"How many times did he butt her?"

Hester and Emma looked at each other. Emma said, "Four times? Five?"

Hester nodded.

My heart sank. This was a thousand pound bull. No one could have survived that much punishment.

"She never cried out?" I said. "Even the first time?"

They shook their heads.

"She was a helluva woman," I said, but shouldn't have, since it set Monique to wailin'.

"Hush!" Rose cried out. Her back was to us, and she was standin' a mere ten feet away from the bull. I put my hand on Monique's forearm and she quieted down enough for me to hear Rose cooin' softly at the bull. She was speakin' some sort of language I'd never heard before.

"What's going to happen?" Hester whispered.

I held up my rifle.

"You'll be safe," I said.

Hester didn't seem so sure, which proved her a good judge of the situation.

"What about Rose?" she said.

I shook my head. Things didn't look good for Rose.

I didn't know what to do. If I made a move toward the bull, he might charge the wagon and knock it over. A bull this size could kill half the camp if he got the women on the ground. But if I did nothin', he would surely kill Rose.

The bull blew a snort and stumbled a few steps. He seemed ill. His tongue was all swole up and hung out the side of his mouth like it was too big to fit. Apart from mating, bulls don't generally rear up on their hind legs like a stallion, but this one tried to do just that. The effort made him fall to the ground, where he rolled around in a dusty panic until he shakily got to his feet. His muscles trembled and twitched, as if he'd experienced a sudden tremor. Then he lowered his head and charged sideways, and gored Scarlett's corpse.

Monique screamed.

In all my time around cattle, I'd never seen a bull act like this. He was crazed, seemed possessed by the devil. When he raised his head, I saw why: foam was drippin' from his mouth.

"What *is* that?" Phoebe whispered.

"Hydrophobia," I said.

In the mountains, on the plains, and especially in the woods, I'd seen Rose do a hundred things no one else could do. I'd trust her to survive a winter in the wilderness ahead of any trapper or mountain man. But she and I both knew she weren't gonna talk this bull down. It was gonna charge, no two ways about it.

I could only think of one thing to do, and it wasn't gonna work. But I had to do *somethin'*. I jumped into the wagon, hopin' not to distract the bull 'til I could punish him for bein' distracted. I stood on the seat next to Phoebe so I could squeeze off a shot from the highest possible angle.

I raised my rifle to my cheek.

Rose turned her head and gave me a look that weren't fright, but it weren't confidence, neither. She seemed confounded, like for the first time since I'd known her, she'd didn't have a solution for the problem. She shifted her gaze behind me, as if somethin' was approachin' from the rear. So intense was her look, I turned my head for a split second, to see if Hannah was back there.

But I saw nothin'.

The bull snorted, and pawed the ground again. Behind me, Major whinnied.

Rose locked her eyes on mine and set her jaw. Rose ain't the type that needs to rely on anyone else, but now, seconds away from death, I felt like, for once, she was relyin' on me.

You don't bring down a crazed Longhorn bull with a single shot, and there wouldn't be time for two. My only chance was to hit him in such a manner that Rose could get out of the way when he charged.

And that didn't seem possible.

Unless...

I've shot some buffalo in my day, and bear, too. And I learned there's only one shot that can stop 'em in their tracks.

The heart shot.

Like a buffalo, a bear's heart is big, but well-protected by its shoulder and leg. You can't shoot low, or forward, or you'll have a wounded, angry bear to deal with. I 'spect Texas Longhorn bulls are built similar to buffalo and bears, and would be just as surly if shot poorly. But if I could get this Longhorn to turn his head slightly and take a step forward, he'd expose the area I needed to hit. Unfortunately, even a heart-shot buffalo can run a hundred yards before dyin'. And while a bull ain't exactly a buffalo or bear, this was one helluva big Longhorn, and I'd be awful damn lucky to kill it with one shot in such a way that Rose could get away.

And one shot is all I figured to have.

The bull cocked his head at Rose and pawed the ground one last time before chargin'.

I was standin' on the bench, surrounded by snifflin' whores who I hoped were tryin' hard not to cause movement in the wagon. Time seemed to stand still while I waited for the bull to turn sideways enough for me to shoot his heart.

At that precise moment, several things happened at the same time.

Shrug appeared from the far side of the trail, and hurled a rock at the bull's face.

The bull charged Rose, but turned sideways a split second when Shrug's rock hit him.

I fired my rifle.

In the space of a heartbeat, two things were clear. First, I'd made a perfect shot. And second, it didn't make a difference.

The bull never slowed as it attacked Rose.

And that didn't matter either.

Because by the time the bull got to where Rose had been standing...she was no longer there.

CHAPTER 31

EVERYTHIN' HAPPENED SO fast, it seemed a blur. The bull stopped a few feet beyond where he would have gored Rose, had she been there, and now he looked around, stupefied, tryin' to locate her. I took that opportunity to squeeze off another shot to his heart, and two more to his lung. The bull shuddered twice, took a step toward Shrug, then buckled to his knees, and fell.

Phoebe shouted, "Wayne!"

I lowered my rifle and swept the area with my eyes, lookin' for Rose.

"Was she gored?" I said.

"She just...disappeared!" Leah said.

Apparently Mary hadn't seen Shrug 'til that moment, because she suddenly yelled, "What in the name of God *is* that thing? *Shoot* it, Emmett!"

Phoebe jumped out of the wagon and ran toward him. They embraced briefly, which caused Mary to say, "What is she *doing*? Hugging it?"

I said, "That's Shrug. He saved her life recently."

"*Jesus*!" she said.

Shrug and Phoebe realized everyone was watchin' 'em. They backed away from each other, suddenly self-conscious about their public display. Then Shrug ran to check on Scarlett. As he turned her over, Phoebe shouted, "She's alive!"

There was more. Little Hannah was underneath her, safe and sound.

I put my rifle in the wagon, and we all ran over to see.

Scarlett had always been a big gal. Bein' unconscious made her heavier still. But me and Shrug and the women managed to get her in the wagon anyway. She was in bad shape and gettin' worse, and I only had one hope for her survival.

"Where's Rose?" I said. "Anyone see what happened to her?"

Shrug looked where she'd been, then up in the sky, then back at me, and shrugged.

"She was standin' there one minute," Leah said, "and the next...she was gone."

"She's a witch," Mary said. "I knew it the minute I met her, and nothing's happened to change my mind ever since. Especially this."

"She must a' got hit by the bull," I said. "She's slight, and could've been butted a good distance. Let's spread out and check the grass on the other side of the trail. Maybe she got knocked into a hole or somethin'."

"Someone should stay in the wagon with Scarlett and Hannah," Phoebe said. I noticed she was strokin' Hannah's hair. It seemed to calm her.

"How about you stay with her then," I said.

Phoebe nodded.

I looked at Hannah. She hadn't said a word, had no expression on her face.

"What's wrong with her?" I said.

"She's in shock."

"Will she be okay?"

"Would *you* be?"

I didn't answer, but figured I probably would, had I gotten this far, like Hannah had. Whatever terrible things had befallen this tragic girl, she seemed to weather it pretty well. In the shit hole that was Hannah's life, this was just another turd.

"We'll hope for the best," I said.

From behind us a voice called out, "We'll take your whores, now, and your water, and any money you got."

We turned to find four gunmen on horses enterin' the camp. One had a pearl-handled six-shooter in his hand, and he was aimin' it at the center of my chest. The others had shotguns trained on Shrug and the women.

The guy with the handgun did the talkin'. He was slim and sat tall in the saddle, and had on a brown derby hat. His eyes were enormous, twice the size of a normal man's, and crazy lookin'. They put me in mind of a stone killer named Bose Rennick, who used to travel with Sam Hartman. Hartman was a regular curly wolf, often considered the cruelest man who ever lived. I'd seen Bose once, six years ago, when I was ridin' through Jacksboro, Texas. He was chained to a tree on the edge of town, with three lawmen guardin' him. I only saw him a few seconds that day, but he had the same giant and crazy-lookin' eyes as this hombre. Somehow Bose managed to escape from Jacksboro, and he and Sam lit out for Mexico, where they raised a ruckus 'til the Federales threw 'em in prison. I heard they were killed tryin' to break out, which meant the guy in front of me weren't him.

But that didn't make his eyes any less frightenin' than Bose Rennick's. If there was anythin' on the other side of this man's eyes, well, he weren't sharin' it with the rest of us.

The first time he'd spoke, his voice was rough and scratchy. This time it was clear as a bell, and the words came out of his mouth rich and deep, and sounded like they'd been basted in honey. It was far and away the nicest voice I ever heard on a man.

"I'm Bose Rennick," he said. "And this here's Sam Hartman."

"Never heard a' you," I said.

Sam Hartman pulled the hammer back on his shotgun. He looked–not just eager, but like he couldn't wait to pull the trigger. I thought about the look in Rose's eyes just before the bull charged her. She must have seen, or sensed these fellers comin' up behind us.

Bose cast a watchful eye on Shrug. His eyebrow went up.

"What the fuck happened to him?" he said, his voice as sweet as if he'd sung the words. You hear Bose Rennick's voice and decide the good Lord must a' felt the need to make it up to him for puttin' them double-sized crazy eyes on his face.

Sam Hartman said, "Who gives a shit about the cripple?" To me, he said, "You and him, get the dead one and the kid outta the wagon. Then hitch it up and put the whores in it, and two of the water barrels."

"Them barrels are mostly empty," I said.

Bose flipped his gun toward the supply wagon as casually as I might shoo a fly, and shot a hole in one of the barrels. When no water spurted out, he said, "You got water somewhere."

"We've got some," I said.

"Put what you have in the wagon, along with your canteens," he said.

"We'll be needin' them canteens for our journey," I said.

Sam and Bose looked at each other.

"I'm afraid your journey has come to an end," Bose said.

I marveled at the man's voice. It was so full and deep and rich, it would almost be worth getting' shot just to hear him talk about it afterward.

Almost.

I glanced at Shrug, but he seemed fresh out of ideas. I kicked a clod off the bottom of my boot and looked back up at Bose Rennick.

"You got a damn fine voice, Mr. Rennick," I said.

"Fuck you!"

No doubt about it, we were in a bad way.

I'd left my six gun and derringer in my saddlebag last night. I would've had the derringer, but was afraid I might accidentally shoot Gentry while rollin' around on the ground with her. So I was unarmed, Shrug was on the wrong side of the shotguns, and Rose had disappeared into thin air. The only thought that gave me comfort was knowin' Gentry was still on the hill, safe and sound. While she didn't have much frontier experience, she was resourceful. If worse came to worse, she ought to be able to make her way back to Springfield.

As if readin' my mind, Bose motioned toward the hill where Gentry and I laid together fifteen minutes earlier.

"There ain't but three trees on that hill," Bose said, "but your yaller-faced girlfriend is tied to one of 'em. Earl Grubbs is fuckin' her at the moment, but in ten minutes, if we ain't back, his orders are to shoot her."

I wanted to rush him. If I did, would he and the others be startled enough to start shootin'? If I could draw their fire, maybe Shrug would have enough time to pull some stones from his pouch. Shrug was fast and deadly, and he might be able to kill one or two of 'em and get away. If that happened, he might be able to save the women. Maybe Gentry, too.

It weren't a great plan, but it was worth a try. They'd kill me, but they were gonna kill me anyway.

As I got ready to make my move, several things went through my mind. I wondered how far I'd get. Would I make it to Rennick's horse? I didn't think so. Bose was a lightning-quick, deadly shooter, and I'd get no more than four feet.

I hesitated.

It was a poor plan. I wouldn't live long enough to draw fire from the other two. Unless I could come up with a way to make all three gunmen concentrate on me.

The odds weren't high, but they weren't impossible, neither.

"Get them outta the wagon or I'll shoot you where you stand," Bose said.

I took a deep breath.

It was now or never.

I reminded myself to turn sideways as I attacked, to give 'em a smaller target. Maybe I'd point at somethin' or shout before runnin' at him. That might distract the others. And Shrug would take the cue, right? Of course he would. He was always alert, always ready.

I looked up at Bose.

That's what I'd do, shout somethin'. Shout somethin', then rush him, fast and furious as possible.

I made my move, and I did manage to get the shout out.

But before I could rush Bose Rennick, all hell broke loose.

CHAPTER 32

IT STARTED WITH Rose, who came from—well, I don't know where the hell she came from, but I felt her hand on my shoulder, and when I turned to look, her mouth was movin' fast as lightnin'.

But no words were comin' out.

She weren't starin' at me or Bose or Sam or the other guy, just straight ahead. I heard Bose yell "What the hell?" and then his horse started twitchin' and shiverin' uncontrollably. Its nostrils flared and its eyes bugged out. Then it reared up. Then the other horses reared. Then they started wheelin' around in tight, fast circles.

I looked at Rose again and had to jump back. Her lips were still makin' silent words, but her eyes had turned yellow, with black pupils that went vertical, like a snake's.

The gunmen tried to calm their horses, but couldn't. The horses were so out of control, the riders had to use both hands just to hang on. Their guns clattered to the ground as they attempted to still their mounts.

But the horses were havin' none of it. For some reason—and I'm pretty sure it had to do with Rose—they were spooked out of their minds. They whinnied and stamped their feet and bucked and spun.

And then, for no reason I could determine, they turned and galloped away, despite their riders' best intentions to make 'em stop.

I looked at Rose. She was still starin' at somethin' I couldn't see.

"Where are they goin'?" I said.

She kept starin' and movin' her lips as though she didn't know I was there. I said, "Rose! What happened with the bull? Where *were* you? How'd you keep from gettin' gored?" But she never responded, never stopped movin' her lips.

There were lots of questions I wanted answers to, but they could wait. Gentry couldn't.

"Watch the women!" I yelled to Shrug, and bolted across the camp toward Major. As I untied his lead I heard Phoebe say, "Why didn't they just jump off their horses?"

I'd wondered the same thing.

I jumped on Major's back. Heard Mary say, "They couldn't."

She was right. It was as if they'd been stuck to their saddles.

"She did it!" Mary yelled, pointin' at Rose. "She's a witch!"

"Shut up, Mary!" Phoebe scolded. "She just saved our lives!"

Had she?

I dug my heels into Major's flanks and forced him up the hill.

CHAPTER 33

BOSE HAD BEEN right about one thing.

There weren't many trees on the hill.

But he was wrong about Earl Grubbs fuckin' Gentry under one of 'em.

Earl was lyin' face down in the grass, dead as a doornail, by Gentry's feet. She was holdin' Earl's horse on a lead line.

"You okay?" I hollered as I rode up to her.

"I'm fine," she said. "How's Scarlett?"

I climbed off my horse. Gentry dropped the lead line and threw her arms around me and held me like I was a post and everythin' around us was a cyclone. Like if she let go, she might get swept away. The poultice on her face was all dry and cracked, and curled in places. It didn't seem to smell half as bad as before.

"How'd you know about Scarlett?" I said.

Her face was in my coat, so her words came out muffled. "Rose told me."

"What?"

"Rose told me."

"What? When?"

"Couple minutes ago."

I pulled away from her.

"What are you *talkin'* about?" I said.

She looked at me like I was daft.

"Rose said Scarlett got hurt. You just left the camp, right? So I'm askin' if she's okay."

I shook my head.

"She ain't. But she's alive."

"Thank God."

"What do you mean you saw Rose just now?"

"I didn't see her. I—" she seemed confused.

"You what?" I said.

"I—I don't know. I—someone was telling me those things. In my head. It sounded like Rose's voice, and it seemed quite normal at the time. But...now that I'm saying it out loud...it...sounds crazy."

It did sound crazy.

"Did he hurt you?" I said.

"He grabbed me a bit. But not for long."

"How'd you kill him?"

"Stabbed him."

"With what?"

"I keep a knife in my dress," she said. "I wiped it off already, on his pant leg." She studied my face a moment and said, "Are *you* okay?"

"Of course."

"Then hadn't we better ride down the hill and see about Scarlett?"

I wondered if maybe she was in shock over what had happened to her. I mean, Rose couldn't have been gored by a bull in the valley one second and talkin' to Gentry the next. This tree was a half mile from where the bull had been.

"Did Rose happen to say anythin' else?"

"She said she was checkin' on me."

"And you spoke to her?"

She frowned. "Did I dream it?"

"I don't know."

I really didn't know. I only knew it made no sense. How did Rose escape the bull? How could she be up here talkin' to Gentry, and down there, scarin' Rennick's horses away?

"You never saw Rose?" I said.

"Nope. I just heard a voice, and then..." she snapped her fingers.

"Then what?"

"It was gone."

I held out my hands, exasperated. "Well, didn't that spook you?" I said.

She gestured at Grubbs. "One minute Monique is screaming, and you run off. Then four riders show up out of nowhere and a bug-eyed lunatic grabs me by the arm and pulls me up on his horse and gallops to this tree. Then he throws me to the ground. This one gets off his horse and pulls a gun on me. The crazy-eyed man tells him to kill me, then him and two others ride down the hill. This one grabs me and says if I don't give him a pop, he's gonna shoot me. He starts pullin' my dress up, and I stab him."

"I figured that out already," I said.

"Well, after dealin' with killers and rapers, why the hell would I'd be spooked by the voice of a witch in my head?"

I took off my hat with one hand and smoothed my hair with the other. Then put my hat back on and said, "That's dangerous talk, callin' someone a witch."

"Oh, come on, Emmett. You know she's a witch. Everyone knows it."

"It's loose talk, is what it is."

Gentry frowned. "Are you serious? The woman is twenty! Forgettin' the fact she claims to have lived with pirates 150 years ago, she's buried six husbands! She sees things comin' that ain't even left where they're coming *from*! She talks to horses! She sniffs truth out of liars! She cooks food for people who ain't showed up yet, and knows how many there'll be for breakfast, and what they like to eat. She can tell who's fornicatin' with who, and knows about titty contests that took place forty miles away. She's a witch, Emmett. A good one, maybe, but a witch all the same."

"There must be a different explanation."

"Well, until we come up with one, she's a witch."

I stared at her a minute.

"You're not jealous of Rose, are you?"

"Of course not!"

"Well, I can see where some might raise an eyebrow over the fact we travel together."

"Oh, hell, Emmett. Anyone can see there's nothin' between you but friendship. You're like brother and sister. An-

Anyways, if she was interested in you, she would've put a love spell on you long ago. And if you were interested in her, she'd have turned you into a newt by now."

I got on Major's back. "You ready to go?"

"What about the dead guy?" she said.

"We'll leave Earl Grubbs to the grubs."

"I'm okay with that," she said.

She climbed on Earl's horse and followed me down the hill.

CHAPTER 34

"HOW'D YOU ESCAPE the bull?"

We were back in camp. Shrug and Phoebe were sittin' with Hannah. Gentry was tellin' her story to the whores as they sat around the stones we'd placed for last night's campfire. Rose and me were in the wagon with Scarlett, who was lyin' face down, stark naked, her face to one side. Her eyes were closed and she was unconscious, a good thing, since Rose was pourin' sting juice on her wounds. Scarlett's back, sides, and butt looked like a battlefield. She had gapin' holes in her body, and where bones should be, I saw horrible bruises formin'. Some of her ribs were clearly broken, but she'd be lucky if that was the worst of it. I'd seen men with lesser wounds who never made it off the doctor's table.

But Scarlett was in the best hands in the West, far as I was concerned. Rose had saved me and several others I'd brought to her for fixin', though none this bad. Still, if anyone could bring Scarlett back to normal, it'd be Rose.

I watched her rummage around in the leather bag she used for her doctorin' supplies. She produced a bottle that had some clear liquid in it, and poured a useful amount on a piece of cloth, handed it to me and said, "Hold this against her nose for five seconds, and again, if she jumps or hollers."

"What is it?"

"Something to keep her asleep while I stitch her up."

I did as told, and watched Rose thread a needle with some sort of thick cord.

"That ain't silk thread," I said.

"Sometimes silk thread isn't enough," she said.

"It smells like tar. What is it?"

"Catgut."

I took a closer look, then lowered my voice so as not to alarm the others. "Do you mean to tell me you're sewin' her up with the guts of an actual cat?"

"Of course not!" she said.

"Well, thank the Lord for that," I said, glad to know she wasn't stayin' up nights carvin' cats.

"I use the intestines of sheep and goats," she said, as she plunged the needle into a partic'larly nasty gash and pulled the catgut through the hole. She worked fast and efficiently, and in no time had the worst wound closed. Then she poured some more sting juice on it.

"You cut that cord out of livestock?" I said.

"It's a natural fiber in the walls of the intestines. I just strip it out, and work it with a cloth 'til it's smooth."

"I never heard of such."

"You'd be amazed how much cord you can get from a single goat," she said. "When I slaughter one for food, I get a year's worth of cord."

"Who knew that about goats," I said. "You kill 'em, and eat 'em, and they wind up savin' your life."

Scarlett moaned, and her body jerked sharply. I put the cloth under her nose again and she went quiet. I watched Rose stitch some more wounds. "Don't them intestines cause infection?"

She gave me a curious look. "Why yes, they do, Emmett. But I soak them in phenol to make them sterile."

"Phenol?"

"It's a chemical. That's where the tar smell comes from."

While Rose worked, I thought about what Mary and Gentry had said about her bein' a witch. I'd known her awhile, and knew she did witchy things, but never considered her a true witch. As one who never believed in witches, how was I supposed to suddenly think of her as one? And if it's true that witches were roamin' the earth, what else would I have to believe? That there's ghosts and goblins and haints? I sure hoped to hell I wouldn't have to deal with a haint someday.

Rose stopped a minute and sighed. "This girl's in trouble." She closed her eyes and lifted her head up, like she needed a break.

"How'd you escape the bull?" I said.

"Don't worry about the bull," she said.

"You were there one minute, the bull charged then you were gone."

"It just appeared that way to you."

"It appeared that way to *all* of us," I said. "Includin' the bull!"

Rose sighed again, lowered her head, opened her eyes. "Let's focus on Scarlett, okay?"

"Fine," I said. But I didn't plan to let the subject die. Not 'til I had some answers.

CHAPTER 35

ROSE FINISHED THE stitchin', poured some more sting juice on the wounds, and shook the dust out of Scarlett's underthings. Then she poured a different kind of liquid on the underthings and pressed them against Scarlett's stitches. She pushed Scarlett onto her side, and made a pillow out of Scarlett's dress and placed it under her cheek. Then she collected her medical supplies and placed 'em in the bag.

"You saved her, didn't you!"

"Not for long."

"What do you mean?"

She shook her head. "There's not much more I can do, under the circumstances."

"How bad is she?"

"Honestly? I don't think she's going to make it."

"She'll make it," I said.

Rose looked at me as if waitin' for an explanation.

"She's hearty," I said.

Rose kept studyin' my face.

"I don't know what else to tell you," I said, "except that the West needs women like Scarlett, and she's the kind of woman that survives."

"She's hurt pretty badly, Emmett."

"I know."

"I've stitched her up as good as I can, and I have what I need to prevent infection. But her stitches are going to burst as soon as the wagon starts moving."

"We can't get where we're goin' without movin' the wagon," I said.

"What she needs is a bed, and someone to care for her."

"That's all?"

"That, and time. It'll take at least six months to heal her broken bones."

"Six months?"

"Assuming her back isn't broken."

"And if it is?"

"She'll never walk again."

"Shit," I said.

We were quiet a moment.

"You like her," Rose said.

"I do."

"I'm sorry, Emmett. But she won't survive ten minutes riding in this wagon."

"You're positive about that?"

"I am. And she can't ride a horse."

"Well, a' course not."

"And we can't stay here with her."

I nodded.

I looked at the women across the way. Gentry had finished tellin' her tale, and now they were castin' a close watch on Rose. And whisperin'.

I said, "They think you're a witch."

She made a sound that weren't exactly like a laugh, but close to one.

"What's so funny?"

"I've been called worse."

"You have?"

I wondered what worse thing you could call a woman.

"Let it go, Emmett."

"I'm tryin' to, Rose, I surely am. But you seemed to just disappear. Then you showed up, outta nowhere, and spooked them horses like I never seen horses spooked. And Gentry says she heard you speakin' to her in her head, and says you told her about Scarlett."

"Oh, Emmett," she sighed.

"What?"

"Those are just parlor tricks."

"*Parlor* tricks?"

"That's all it was."

"Must be one helluva parlor where you come from," I said.

She put her hands in front of her, elbows at her sides, palms facing up. "Your expertise is the physical world, mine is the metaphysical."

"I have no idea what you're sayin'."

"Trickery."

"What about it?"

"It's not your strong suit. Remember the fish in the water barrel?"

"You heard me tell that story? You couldn't have! You were in the other wagon!"

"You've told that story a dozen times since I've known you. And you never figured it out."

That was true.

"So you ain't a witch?"

"Don't be ridiculous," she said.

I pointed at the others. "Well, *they* think you are. And that could be a problem."

"You think so?"

"I do."

"Then maybe you should ask them."

That took me by surprise. "What do you mean?"

"I bet they'll only remember that Scarlett got gored by a bull, and you shot it, and Gentry killed a man and took his horse."

I looked across the way and noticed the women had stopped lookin' at Rose. Nor were they whisperin' about her, best I could tell.

"How'd you do that?" I said.

"Memory's a funny thing," Rose said.

"Maybe it's a tricky thing," I said.

She smiled.

"What about Shrug?" I said.

"You and Shrug will have your own thoughts about what happened."

"How come we won't forget?"

"It's important you know those men in case you see them next year in Dodge City."

"You think we'll see 'em again next year?"

She smiled. "What am I, a witch?"

CHAPTER 36

SCARLETT LET OUT a low moan.

"You think her back's broken?" I said.

Rose ran her hands up and down Scarlett's spine. "I can't tell," she said. "But it's bad. If she lives, she'll never be the same."

Phoebe and Shrug were sittin' together. She was holdin' Hannah in her arms like a girl might hold a giant doll, and Shrug was puttin' on a helluva show for her, jugglin' four rocks with one hand while slappin' the top of his head with the other. But Hannah didn't so much as smile.

"Is Scarlett gonna wind up lookin' like Shrug?"

"No one looks like Shrug," Rose said. "He's a walking miracle. But if Scarlett survives, she'll walk poorly and have constant pain in her life. And countless other problems."

"Like what?"

Rose shook her head. "She'll never birth a child, for one thing."

"Will she be able to whore?"

Rose grimaced. "I won't even dignify that question with a response."

"I just meant–"

"I *know* what you meant."

"No, really. I was just wonderin' if she'd be able to earn a livin'."

"*Shame* on you!" she said.

I lowered my head. Rose had a way of makin' me feel bad when I didn't even know why I should. All I was doin' was thinkin' about the woman's welfare. Speakin' of which, I suddenly had an idea.

"You remember Molly Snow?"

Rose stopped bein' put out with me long enough to cock her head. "Of course. What about her?"

"Molly's place ain't far from here. Maybe Scarlett could hang on 'til then. Molly would welcome the company, and Scarlett might be able to mend if she were in a bed and cared for by Molly."

She thought a moment. "That's got to be forty miles."

I pointed to the north-west horizon. "If we cut straight through it'd be less than twenty."

She looked where I'd pointed. "How much less?"

"Hard to say, exactly."

"Best guess."

"Eighteen miles, maybe less."

"If we head straight there, we'll miss Copper Lake," she said.

"We could take Scarlett to Molly's, then come back to fill the water barrels."

Rose bit her lip, thinkin' about it. She looked at Scarlett.

"I'm serious, Emmett. She won't survive the wagon ride."

"What if I make a lean-to and drag her behind Major? I could get to Molly's by dusk, drop Scarlett off, and ride back. I could do the whole trip in"—I paused to calculate—"six hours."

"Even a lean-to would be too rough a ride," Rose said. "However..."

I waited.

"What if we tied the lean-to between the two horses?"

"I can't trust Earl's horse not to buck or kick," I said. "And if he does, that would be worse than haulin' Scarlett in the wagon."

Rose thought a minute, then said, "Four of us could take her. One person leads the horse, two walk behind carrying the lean-to. We could take turns."

"That's a lot of liftin' and carryin'. What would the fourth person do?"

"Ride the second horse."

I stared at her a second. Then said, "Right. Because we'll need two horses to get us all back."

She nodded.

"That's good plannin'," I said.

"Well, it's not perfect."

"Why not?"

"We don't even know if Molly is still there."

"'Cause of the draught?"

"Uh huh."

"She and Paul are close enough to Copper Lake to stay stocked. It ain't likely they'd abandon their ranch due to water trouble."

We were quiet a minute. I don't know what she was thinkin', but I was calculatin' how much weight two people would have to lift and carry, and how long each would have to do it.

"Shrug should stay here," I said.

"I agree. Shrug can take care of the others. You and I will have to go because we'll need your strength. And I need to care for Scarlett along the way. When we get there, I'll need to teach Molly how to care for her."

"We can take Major, and Earl Grubbs's horse."

Rose nodded. "And Monique."

"What?"

"We'll need to take Monique."

"Ain't gonna work," I said. "Apart from you, she's the slightest woman in camp."

"So?"

"The lean-to will run at least a hundred pounds. Scarlett's one-eighty if she's an ounce."

"Monique will carry her end."

"There's better choices."

"She loves her, Emmett."

"Well, a'course she does. We *all* love Scarlett."

"No, Emmett. I mean, she *loves* Scarlett."

"Huh?"

"They're lovers."

As the full meanin' of her words hit me, I felt like I'd been cold-cocked. I took my hat off, ran my hand over my head, and stared at my hat a full minute before puttin' it back on.

"You mean to tell me–"

"How could you not know?" she said.

CHAPTER 37

SHRUG GUARDED HANNAH and Scarlett while the rest of us went up the hill and gathered wood from around the three trees. I cut a dozen lengths of rope from Earl Gruggs's lasso, and passed 'em around so the women could help me lash the wood together. With so many helpin' hands, it only took two hours to build a decent lean-to. When it was finished, I dragged it down the hill behind Major and we lifted Scarlett onto it, and tied her down while Rose held Major's lead line.

The rest of us stood there, lookin' at the lean-to.

"Monique," I said.

Monique walked over and stood behind the pole on the right side. I took my spot at the left, counted to three, and to my surprise, Monique lifted her end three feet off the ground. We stood there for twenty seconds, then I told Rose to lead Major ten paces. She did. When Rose came to a stop, I nodded at Monique, and we set the lean-to down gently.

So beloved was Scarlett, all the women—Gentry, Phoebe, Leah, Emma, Hester, and even Mary—volunteered to ride Earl's horse and take turns carryin' the lean-to. When I chose Phoebe, Shrug gave me a stern look. I walked over to him and put my hand on his shoulder. He pushed it off and glared at me. I motioned for him to walk with me away from the camp so the others couldn't hear.

"If you don't want her to go, just say so. But I think it's important for Phoebe to see what pioneer life is really like. I don't think she has any idea what she's in for with Hiram Pickett, stuck in a sod house on a dirt ranch in the middle a' nowhere. But seein' how Molly and Paul live oughta give her a good idea."

Shrug weighed my words a minute, then nodded. I turned away, intendin' to walk back to camp. Shrug put his hand on my shoulder to stop me.

I turned, half expectin' him to hit me, but instead, he reached into his pouch and handed me a single stone. When I took it, he looked down at the ground to show me he was sorry for the way he'd acted.

"No offense taken," I said. "You're my best friend, right?"

He nodded.

"And I'm yours, right?"

He made a face, and shook his head no.

I laughed. "Kiss my ass!"

Shrug grinned, and we walked back to camp.

We decided Shrug and the women would continue without us to Copper Lake and fill the barrels as best they could. Then we'd meet up in Kansas, at Blackstrap Crick, which I knew would be dry. Phoebe, Rose and Monique filled a dozen canteens and packed what supplies we'd need for the trip, which I now figured would take three days.

Before leavin', Phoebe walked over and said somethin' to Shrug, and he nodded at her. From the look on his face, I'd guess she told him she was gonna miss him. Then she hugged Hannah goodbye, and kissed the top of her head. She climbed on Earl's horse, and off we went, under a cloudless sky, headin' for the little sod house outside Maynard, Kansas, where me and Rose delivered Molly Thomas to her mail order husband, Paul Snow, six months earlier.

CHAPTER 38

THERE'S NO COMFORTABLE way to carry two hundred and eighty pounds of lean-to and lady over uneven terrain, even with Major handlin' his half of the load.

The closest you can get is to stand straight, with your arms hangin' naturally, so you can hold the pole at your lowest point without bendin' over. Unfortunately, there were two of us carryin' the thing, and we were different heights. Bein' much taller, I had to bend over the whole time and lift the lean-to with my arms bent, which quickly put a strain on my neck, shoulders, forearms and elbows, and a kink in my back. Every step hurt worse than the one before, and we couldn't find a walkin' rhythm, due to all the stumblin' we did.

After a few minutes, Scarlett came to and cried out in pain. Monique grew excited, and called out to her in French. But Scarlett failed to answer, and Monique turned gloomy.

Both Rose and Phoebe spoke French better than Scarlett, and tried to engage Monique in conversation to keep her spirits up. Since Rose was walkin' twenty feet ahead of us, leadin' Major, Phoebe did most of the talkin', which amounted to reassurin' Monique that Scarlett would be okay, and lettin' her know we cared deeply for her, and were gonna do all we could to help her. Monique let out a stream of French words in response. When I asked what she said, Rose answered, "Monique is amazed that Phoebe, a proper woman, volunteered for such a hard task. She's even more amazed that Phoebe cares about Scarlett, a common whore, and said she'd never forget her kindness."

"Don't she know you're a proper woman too?" I called out to Rose.

"According to you, she probably thinks I'm a witch," Rose said, laughing. Then she said, "It makes sense she'd single Phoebe out for her gratitude. After all, you and I are getting paid for making the journey. As a paying customer, Phoebe has gone far out of her way to be of service."

"That she has," I agreed.

I turned to look at Phoebe, but she pretended not to hear the compliments. But it was true. Phoebe was an exceptional Easterner, and though her tongue could be sharp and her stand on cussin' severe, I'd come to respect her for far more than her looks and coffee.

Deflectin' the conversation, Phoebe said, "So Paul and Molly are newlyweds?"

"Well, they're recently married," I said.

"Isn't that the same thing?"

I laughed. "They ain't likely to put you in mind of newlyweds."

"Why not?"

I thought about how best to say it. "Neither of 'em are partic'larly good with people."

"Perhaps they're good together."

"I hope so."

"Why do you say that?"

"Well, Paul's an odd duck, and Molly's a sharp-tongued nag."

"They sound like a rather unpleasant sort."

"To you and me, maybe. But it takes a certain temperament to live in poverty, away from people. They're probably a good fit. If he ain't killed her by now."

"I'm sure that's just an expression, meant to amuse me."

"Did it?"

"No. I don't find any facet of this situation amusing. You're the one who brought her west to live with Paul. If they were mismatched you shouldn't have left her there."

"I didn't make her stay. It was her choice. And anyway, odd as he is, I think she's the one got the bargain, if there's one to be had."

"So you think they're happy?"

"Happy?"

"Aren't newlyweds supposed to be happy?"

"If there *had* been any happy," I said, "it probably wore off by suppertime."

We trudged on.

As a former gunfighter, horseman, and buffalo hunter, I wasn't used to this type of travel. My muscles kept lockin' up on me and I was afraid my arms might go numb and I'd drop my corner of the lean-to. Because I had to walk in such an awkward position, I tried to find a way to stretch my neck and shoulders while carryin' my part of the load. But nothin' worked.

We got a mile and a half before takin' our first break, which lasted long enough for Monique to pour some water on Scarlett's hair and wash her face. She traded places with Phoebe. Rose took a funnel from her bag and poured canteen water through it into Scarlett's mouth. I stretched my back for a couple of minutes, and we went at it again, with Phoebe on the left corner this time, and me on the right. I hoped it would help my back to rotate positions each time we stopped, but I feared I was only givin' the lean-to a different angle to punish me.

For a city woman, Phoebe was strong. Like Monique, she made no complaints. But the goin' was slow, and gettin' slower, due to the painful nature of our journey. It weren't just the weight of the lean-to that was breakin' us down, it was a combination of things, like the numbness in our necks, shoulders and lower backs and the blisters under our gloves and inside our boots. Had we been tryin' to cross a mountain, or even a series of hills, we couldn't a'done it. But we were on the plains, just past the Kansas border, and the land was flat and mostly grass, far as the eye could see.

Not that the grass was green, or fun to walk through, 'cause it weren't. It was brown and brittle, like over-cured hay, and crunched under our feet like crusted snow. I'd never seen grass this dry. Even our horses wouldn't eat it! But dead as it was, the grass was still thick and long enough to to cover most of the surface holes you'll find on prairie land. Where it was patchy, we came upon hard-as-rock dirt clods that bruised our blistered feet.

"Did Mr. Pickett happen to tell you what type of material his house was made of?" I asked Phoebe, two miles into the trip.

"He did not," she said. "Nor did I ask."

The scent of urine filled the air, which told us Scarlett's bladder was workin' properly.

"Shouldn't we stop and clean her up?" Phoebe said.

"Under normal circumstances, I'd say yes. But we haven't covered much ground, and can't afford to take the time. And anyway, because of how the lean-to is slanted, her upper body's higher than her privates, meanin' her piss ain't likely to get in her wounds."

"It's barbaric," Phoebe said. "A woman shouldn't be forced to lie in her own urine."

"There's worse things," I said. "Like livin' in a sod house, for instance."

Phoebe said, "I've always held the opinion that it's not *where* you live, but *how* you live that counts."

From up ahead I heard Rose chuckle.

"Well, I s'pect Mr. Pickett's got a sod house," I said.

We walked a few steps without speakin'.

"And what if he does?" Phoebe said.

"You know much about sod houses?"

"I've never heard that expression before, in reference to a house."

I didn't know what she meant by *expression,* so I didn't speak again until I hollered, "Rose? We've got a situation back here."

"What's wrong?" Rose said.

"Scarlett just shit herself."

CHAPTER 39

AFTER WE SET the lean-to down, Rose said, "Turn away, Emmett, while I clean Scarlett up." To Phoebe she said, "After I'm finished, you can lead Major, and I'll take a turn carrying the lean-to."

Before Rose could get started on Scarlett, Monique jumped off her horse and insisted on doin' the cleanin'. Rose allowed her to, but kept a close watch. Afterward, she checked Scarlett's wounds.

"How's she holdin' up?" I said.

"I don't like what I saw," Rose said.

"What's that?"

"Her scat was almost black."

I knew that to be a bad sign. Meant she might've busted somethin' inside her.

"Is that why she's unconscious all the time?" I said. "Is she in a coma?"

"No. I've severely drugged her. Otherwise, she'd be in such pain I doubt she'd survive the trip."

We headed onward.

Rose was small, but sturdy, and she got us a mile closer to Molly's place before needin' to stop. We rotated positions again, and journeyed on. After our next short break, Phoebe and Monique traded places. By then we'd walked an agonizing six miles.

"Most folks don't live on the plains for a reason." I said.

"And what reason is that?" Phoebe said.

"Actually, there's a lot of reasons. But one is a lack of trees. Since lumber's scarce, people often dig squares of grass out of the ground and stack 'em up in a big pile and build a house out of it."

I wasn't sayin' all this to be mean. I'd brought a number of women out west only to see the look on their faces when they realized what they were up against.

"The squares are about eight inches thick, with grass on top and packed dirt beneath it that's held together by roots," I said. "Among the roots you'll find all sorts of crawly bugs, the worst of which is chiggers."

She didn't respond, so I said, "You know much about chiggers?"

With frost in her voice, she said, "I learned more about chiggers than I cared to when living among them in a cave recently."

"In your sod house, if you're lucky, you might have a leaky window or two in the upper curves, to let in some light. You'll also have a stove with a pipe attached to it that goes up through the roof to let out most of the soot."

"Well, I assume Mr. Pickett's house is made of wood and has windows and a veranda," she said.

"A what?"

"A covered porch," she said.

"A porch?"

"I envision a wide, wooden porch with a handrail that wraps elegantly around the front of the house, where people can sit and rock while enjoying conversation."

Rose stifled a laugh.

I said, "Fuel's a problem."

"Why's that?" Phoebe said.

"I've known plains people to travel forty miles to find wood that ain't hardly fit to burn."

Phoebe said, "I'd like to believe that Mr. Pickett is a prudent man, and one who would have an adequate supply of firewood for his stove at all times."

"Well, if he don't have much firewood stocked up, he'll still be fine, I s'pect."

"And why is that?" she said.

"Well, you said Pickett's a rancher, so if he's got cows you'll have your fuel. Assumin' the cows ain't dead from the draught and still have grass or hay to eat."

"What do the cows have to do with fuel?"

"They shit large piles of manure, what we call cow chips. When the shit pile dries, the settlers stack it inside the house and use it for fuel."

"You're joking."

"I ain't."

"I should think the stench would be horrific!" she said.

"Actually, it burns cleaner than you might think. Of course, if Mr. Pickett's got hay, he might let you spend a good part of each day twistin' it into bundles and stackin' it in your sod house."

"Yes, well as I say, I'm certain Mr. Pickett's home is made of the finest wood money can buy."

"Yes, ma'am."

"I don't like your tone, Mr. Love, nor do I approve of the assumptions you've made about my fiancé."

"Well, we'll see when we get there. I hope he's got a fine wood house, 'cause sod houses are fiercely cold in the winter, and scorchin' hot in the summer. And they leak like crazy whenever it rains, which ain't often enough. But when it *does* rain, it won't stop. As the water comes through the sod, it turns the dirt into mud, at which point you and your husband and kids'll be wearin' half the house on your faces and clothes. But you can always rebuild your house, and the good news is, the more often it caves in on you, the better you'll get at fixin' it.

Phoebe was silent awhile. Finally she said, "If you're mocking me, shame on you, since I've done nothing to warrant it. But if you're being serious, I can see why it might be a hard life for a woman, particularly an Easterner, such as myself, who is ill-prepared to suddenly step into such a harsh lifestyle. On the other hand, if a man and women are in love, I'm sure they can overcome all sorts of hardships, including those you've taken the time to catalogue for me."

"I s'pect you're right," I said. "And it's a good thing, because there's a lot more obstacles involved."

"Such as?"

"Well, insects—spiders in partic'lar—love sod houses. Of course, your grass snakes and mice feel right at home in sod, too. On the plus side, if you've got a cat that's a good mouser, he'll stay fat and happy without your havin' to feed him."

"Anything else you may have forgotten to say?"

"Well, if you've studied up on prairie life, you probably know sod folk don't generally have outhouses. But you needn't worry about privacy, since your neighbors are likely to live at least five miles away. You'll spend weeks each year dealin' with head lice, but when they're finally gone it'll be flea and tick season. Regardless of the season you'll have body lice suckin' your blood by day, and bedbugs by night. And if that ain't enough—"

"Mr. Love?" Phoebe said.

"Yes ma'am?"

"Kindly shut up."

CHAPTER 40

EVERYTHIN' AROUND US seemed dead. There weren't a dragonfly, grasshopper, or jackrabbit to be found anywhere among the parched earth. With all the snake holes we'd seen and prairie dog holes we'd tripped in, you'd think we would've seen a few by now. But no. The whole area was so dry I doubted there'd be so much as a drop of dew on the grass tomorrow mornin'.

I looked up. The position of the sun told me it was about four hours past noon, which didn't seem possible after all we'd been through since dawn. It seemed a week ago instead of this mornin' that Phoebe and I were discussin' the journey. I knew then it'd be a hard trek, but I had no idea it would be this bad.

I'm no stranger to hard work. I've carried river rock a hundred yards to build a fireplace, and spent many a day choppin' and haulin' wood. I cut sheets of ice off a lake one bitter-cold winter, and I've dug a well and more than a few latrines.

But I never felt this type of pain doin' a day's work.

After nine miles, my legs were tremblin' and my lower back felt like someone was drivin' railroad spikes in it. My neck and shoulders burned as if prodded by a hot poker. Phoebe and Monique were bleached white with exhaustion, and only Rose and Earl's horse seemed fresh. Rose took another turn at liftin', and Phoebe had to lead Major, since Monique refused to be anywhere she couldn't see Scarlett's face. An hour later, when Rose tripped and stumbled, I came within an inch of droppin' my side of the lean-to. She apologized twice, and even though she was dog tired, insisted on carryin' her end for another mile. It would a' been better for me if she didn't, since she was so much smaller than the others. When she carried, I had to bend over more than I did with the others. But pitchin' in was important to Rose, so I let her, and we trudged on.

It was after six when we came to a large area of hard-packed dirt.

"We'll camp here," I said, "and save some trip for tomorrow."

We got the lean-to off Major's back and hobbled his legs so he wouldn't stray. I removed his saddle, and gave him some water, and Phoebe and Rose did the same for Earl's horse. Then I got my blanket off Major's back and laid it out on the ground for Scarlett.

As if we hadn't lifted enough that day, the four of us bent to the task of liftin' Scarlett off the lean-to in such a way as not to burst the stitches in her back. We managed it, but I have no idea where we found the strength. Once we had Scarlett on the blanket, Rose and Monique tended to her wounds, put her on her side, and placed a rolled-up blanket under her head, and covered her with two of the extra blankets we'd packed.

"How is she?" Phoebe asked.

"Surprisingly well," Rose said. "The sleep medicine is wearing off, so she ought to be conscious soon."

Monique said somethin' in French. Rose answered, and Phoebe translated for me.

"Monique asked if Scarlett would be able to talk tonight, and Rose said it wouldn't surprise her, though she'd be in pain. Then Rose said she planned to sedate Scarlett again before we retire for the night so her crying won't keep us up."

"What cryin'?" I said.

"When she regains consciousness, she's going to be in a lot of pain," Rose said.

"Don't you have somethin' you can give her for that?"

"The pain medicine is what's keeping her sedated," she said. "By the way, you were right about Scarlett."

"How's that?"

"She's remarkably resilient."

I didn't know the word she used, but I was glad to be right about somethin' for a change. I turned my attention to the horses. Though I trusted Major more than Earl's horse, I considered him lucky not to be lame, and didn't want to put him through another day of carryin' the lean-to. I figured to tie him and Earl's horse to the lean-to that night, since there weren't a tree nor rock in sight. Tomorrow I'd hitch up Earl's horse and let him do the liftin'.

Rose and Monique did what they could for Scarlett, then they started unpackin' the cookin' gear. Phoebe and I headed out across the dirt, lookin' for wood.

"How could there be wood out here if there aren't any trees?" she said.

"Independence, Missouri, is the drop off point for pioneers headin' west," I said.

"So?"

"They come by flatboats down the Missouri River, and take wagons the rest of the way."

"But we're a long way south of Independence, are we not?"

"We are for a fact. But some of the settlers head for Tulsa, and we're only a few miles off the Independence-to-Tulsa trail. Buckboards and wagon trains often travel wide of the mark, to avoid outlaws and Indians. I half s'pect we'll find a wagon wheel or chest of drawers someone abandoned along the trail."

Pointin' to the west side of the dirt patch, I said, "Let's check the grass on that side. If we don't find any wood, we can pull enough dried grass out of the ground to make a fast-burnin' fire, and that'll be a whole lot better than no fire at all."

When we got to the grassy area, we fanned out and searched a wide area. I didn't see anythin', so I started pulling up grass. I was about to have Phoebe carry a load back to camp when I heard her say somethin' in a voice so low I couldn't understand what she'd said. I asked her to repeat it. When she didn't, I walked over to where she was standin'.

"What did you say?"

"I said I found some wood," she said, softly.

She was standing solemnly, starin' down at two small sticks, arranged in a cross...that marked a child's grave.

I removed my hat.

Phoebe sighed a heavy sigh. "What do you suppose happened?"

I shook my head. "Could be any of a hundred things."

"I know that, Emmett," she said sharply. "Of *course* there are a hundred—no, a *thousand* things out here on the prairie that can kill a child, sap a man's strength, or destroy a woman's resolve. But give me just five, will you?"

"Ma'am?"

"Tell me the five things you think are the most likely to have killed this poor child."

I'd never had such a strange request asked of me, so I thought powerful hard on it before offerin' up my answer.

"Cholera, typhoid, brain fever, and uncontrollable diarrhea are possible. But if I had to make a guess, I'd say this child fell out of a wagon and got crushed by either the ox or the wheel of the wagon that followed it."

She stared at me. "That *cannot* be a common way to die on the prairie."

"I'm afraid it's quite common," I said.

She grimaced, closed her eyes tightly, and shook her head. "And not one of the diseases you mentioned?"

"No ma'am."

She opened her eyes. "Why not?"

I gestured to the open area all around us and said, "No other graves."

"What about a stampede?"

"Not likely."

"Indians? Outlaws?"

"No, ma'am."

"Why not?"

"Same answer. There ain't but one grave."

"Snakebite?"

"Not too many poisonous snakes in this area."

"God in heaven," she said.

I didn't know what to say to that, so I just stood there holdin' my hat 'til she decided to speak again.

"Such a senseless way to die," she said, finally.

I nodded, privately wonderin' why she cared which way this unknown child might a' died. But then she said somethin' so bizarre it nearly struck me dumb. What she said was, "Should we go ahead then, and take the wood?"

CHAPTER 41

WE DIDN'T TAKE the cross.

Instead, we gathered up some bundles of grass and twisted them into small stacks and tied 'em tight with twine to slow down the burnin'. We didn't have any tools to dig out a pit, so I dismantled a couple of small branches we'd used in the lean-to so we'd have somethin' to set our fryin' pan on. But none of us felt like eatin' just then, despite the fact we were starvin', and needed the nourishment.

We were just too damned tired.

For the next half hour the four of us did nothin' more than relieve ourselves and lie on our backs to stretch. After awhile I took my shirt off and Rose rubbed me down with liniment. I put my shirt back on and looked the other way while she did the same for Monique and Phoebe. Rose claimed not to need any liniment for herself, and I believed her, though I'd a' been more than happy to rub it on her.

I removed a flask from my saddlebag, took a long pull, and passed it around to the others. Then I got the fire goin'. By and by, Rose put some beans and salt pork in the pan, and we commenced to talkin' about how we were dreadin' the last six or eight miles of the trip tomorrow.

When the food was done, Scarlett opened her eyes and said, "What's for dinner?"

CHAPTER 42

MONIQUE SQUEALED WITH delight and raced over to her friend before the rest of us even got to our feet. We let the two of 'em jabber at each other awhile before walkin' over, so as not to intrude.

"She's asking about Hannah," Phoebe said.

"They're usin' a lot of words if that's all they're talkin' about," I said.

Phoebe and Rose exchanged a look. Rose said, "There's a lot of emotions being shared, Emmett. As I mentioned earlier, they're quite close."

After a few minutes, Monique called us over. When we got there, Scarlett was wincin'.

"You're in a great deal of pain," Rose said.

"I feel like I've been drug across the country by horse," she said, forcin' a smile.

"Do you feel like eating something?" Phoebe said.

"If it's not too much trouble," Scarlett said, "I'd like some bull nuts."

We all had a good laugh over that, except for Monique, who didn't understand a word she'd said. Scarlett repeated her comment in French, and Monique shook her head as though it weren't very funny.

When Rose asked about her condition, Scarlett said she couldn't feel nothin' from the waist down, and wondered if that was on account of the drugs. Rose bit her lip and said that was probably it, but we all knew Scarlett had been paralyzed.

Rose said, "Your outside wounds will heal. But I'm concerned about what's happening on the inside. I know you've broken some ribs, and possibly ruptured some organs. What I'm worried about is internal bleeding."

"It hurts when I breathe," Scarlett said. "But that's the only pain I can report. Also, I feel foggy, and sorta like I'm half dreaming."

"That's the drugs," Rose said. "I'll give you another dose after you eat."

"In the meantime, would you like a sip of whiskey?" I said.

Scarlett smiled. "You buying?"

"I am!"

"In my experience," Scarlett said, "a cowboy who shares his whiskey instead of his pecker is a rare find!"

We spent the next hour feedin' Scarlett, and tellin' her about Molly and Paul Snow, and what they were like, and how we expected to be at their place by noon the next day.

"It's a huge imposition," Scarlett said. "I don't feel right about forcing them to take me in."

Monique said somethin', and Phoebe said, "Monique intends to stay at the Snow residence and care for Scarlett until she's ready to travel again."

Rose and I looked at each other.

"It ain't much of a residence," I said.

"Is it a sod house?" Phoebe said. "If so, I'm keen to see it."

"It is for a fact. And the inside's about the size of two wagons set side by side."

"I'm inclined to ask Molly and Paul to let them both stay," Rose said. "Despite the inconvenience."

"You think they'll take on two extra people in that tiny space for six months?"

"I'll pay them so well, they'll have to say yes."

"With what?"

"Medicine."

Medicine bein' the ultimate currency out west.

"That'd do it," I said.

While the rest of us stowed the cookin' gear and tended to the horses, Monique and Scarlett enjoyed some time together. I marveled at their relationship. I'd never heard of such a thing occurrin' between two gals, but I weren't against it. I figure love's a hard enough thing to find, and ought to be treasured however it shows up.

When it became clear that Scarlett was sufferin' terribly, Rose gave her another dose of medicine, and we took turns tellin' her how happy we were that she was feelin' better. She asked if she could be awake durin' the trip the next day, and

Rose said we could give it a try. Scarlett apologized for bein' so heavy, and wished we didn't have to carry her. We explained it was an honor to carry her, and that it had been her size that saved Hannah's life. Scarlett smiled at that. As her eyelids grew heavy, Monique kissed her friend on the forehead.

Before fallin' asleep I couldn't help but remember that just a few hours ago I'd been dreadin' the mornin', because of the effort the trip would require. Now that Scarlett was feelin' better, I found myself lookin' forward to it! And I could tell the others felt the same way. Funny how she had the ability to lift our spirits that way, even though we were terribly sad to learn she'd been paralyzed.

I got to my feet and walked over to where Rose was lyin'.

"What is it, Emmett?"

I whispered, "Scarlett's paralyzed, isn't she?"

She whispered back, "I think so."

"Could she eventually get better and walk again?"

"It's not likely," Rose whispered. "But it's possible."

"I believe she'll walk again," I said.

"I hope so, Emmett."

"Me too."

"Goodnight, Emmett."

"Goodnight, Rose."

When we woke up the next mornin', we learned that Scarlett had died in her sleep.

CHAPTER 43

SCARLETT'S DEATH HIT Monique as hard as anyone I'd ever known who lost a loved one. What made the tragic event even worse, it was Monique who came upon the body. Scarlett's eyes were wide open and her face was twisted into a frightful grimace. A wide river of dried blood ran from her nose and mouth all the way to her waist, and from there, to the parched ground. There was a large stain where the blood had pooled durin' the night before it slowly seeped into the dirt.

It was terrifyin' and sad at the same time, and a sight none of us were likely to forget.

Monique's first reaction surprised me. She jumped on her friend's lifeless body and commenced rainin' blows on it, while screamin' in French. It took two of us to get her off Scarlett, and we both caught kicks and scratches for our trouble. We didn't have the time or strength to deal with

Monique's grief, so Phoebe and I held her down while Rose sedated her.

Much as we wanted to, we couldn't bury Scarlett there. The ground was too hard, and even if it hadn't been, we didn't have a pick or shovel.

"What are we going to do?" Phoebe said.

"We'll have to take her with us," I said.

"Where?"

"To Molly and Paul's house. Paul will have some proper tools, and I'm sure he'll let us bury her on his land somewhere.

"You're not serious," Phoebe said.

"Of course I am!"

"You don't expect us to carry her there, do you?"

"No. We'll tie her to the lean-to, and Earl's horse can drag it. We can be at Molly's in three hours."

I know the women must've cried. If they did, I'm sure I comforted them—but I don't remember it.

I know I must've asked Rose what happened, and why she'd been powerless to prevent it. I'm sure she gave me some sort of medical explanation—but I don't remember that, either.

I know we must've done all the things we had to in order to start the journey, like packin' our blankets, saddlin' the horses, gettin' Scarlett's body onto the lean-to and hitchin' it to Earl's horse—but I don't remember doin' most of 'em. I remember we didn't eat breakfast, and I remember layin' Monique's unconscious body across the saddle on Major's back, and tyin' her to it so she wouldn't fall down. I don't remember coverin' up Scarlett's face with a blanket, but I'm glad one of us thought to do so.

It was only with the most powerful sadness that we left the campsite and began the last stage of our journey, the five or six miles that would take us to Molly and Paul's place. I led the way, towin' Earl's horse as it dragged the lean-to that carried Scarlett's body. Phoebe and Rose followed us, and took turns leadin' Major. We stopped once, when Monique slid off the saddle. On that occasion Rose moved quick as a cat and managed to catch her before she hit the ground. The sensation of fallin' caused Monique to come to, and when she did, she let out a series of heart-wrenchin' sobs that put me in mind of the time when I was a boy and my father was leadin' one of our cows down the road to be butchered, its calf followin' twenty steps behind, bellowin' a mournful bleat.

CHAPTER 44

"I'D OFFER YOU whiskey if I had any," Paul Snow said.

He was eyein' the lean-to. Not because poor Scarlett was still lyin' on it, but because it's the most wood he'd seen in a year. Paul and I were sittin' on a sod bench he'd made the same day he finished buildin' his sod house six years ago. Of course, he'd replaced so many parts of the house and bench over the years, the multi-colored patches looked like checkerboards.

Inside the hut the women had been tendin' to Monique, tryin' to calm her, maybe get her to eat somethin'. But she'd been inconsolable. She was groggy from the sedative, and that was a good thing, 'cause it got her to lie down. But the women were stayin' close, to make sure she didn't do anythin' crazy. Like her husband, Molly knew Scarlett was on the lean-to. But I hadn't got to the part about how I needed a shovel and patch of land so I could bury her.

Normally that would've been the first thing to come out of my mouth, but when we arrived, Monique was threatenin' to kill herself, so I felt it best to have the women give her some attention. I'm sure Scarlett would've been the first person to say her burial could wait a few minutes while we cared for Monique. She wasn't goin' anywhere anyway, bless her soul.

I fetched a flask from my saddlebag and handed it to Paul. He took a long pull, then closed his eyes and sat quietly a minute, enjoyin' the glow a good bourbon will give a man. After a time he said, "Can you spare another sip?"

"It's yours to finish," I said.

"You sure?"

"When I get to Dodge, I s'pect I'll enjoy enough whiskey for ten men."

He nodded. "I envy your destination. Been a long time since I had to kick the shit off my boots to enter a real city."

He sipped his bourbon.

"Damn fine whiskey," he said.

"Ought to be," I said. "It's from Kentucky."

"Do tell."

A couple of skinny chickens were scratchin' the ground in front of us, out of habit, I guessed, since there didn't appear to be any seed there. I noticed Paul's horse was gone.

"You got a shovel somewhere?" I asked. "And a pick?"

"Sorry to say I don't," he said. "I mean, I got a shovel."

"Well, that's somethin'," I said.

"But it's broke," he said.

I gave him a look. "Well then you ain't got a shovel."

"It's a fine shovel," he said. "It's just broke."

I wondered if maybe Paul had been isolated too long.

"How broke is it?" I said.

"The handle's fine."

"Uh huh."

"But it's in two pieces. I'm usin' it to hold our cook pot."

"Why on earth would you bust a perfectly good shovel for that?"

"'Cause the metal part broke into three pieces the year before."

He'd taken me all around the bush with worthless conversation and never scared up a rabbit's worth of sense. I couldn't tell if he was purposely stupid or just plain stupid. Truth is, I didn't know Paul that well. I'd only met him a few hours the day I brought Molly to meet him. She had two papers with her that had been signed by the Maynard Justice of the Peace. I let her and Paul spend three hours together while I took a nap. Then I got her off to the side and asked if she wanted to go through with the marriage. She weren't overly excited about it, but said, "I guess." I told her she had to be sure before I'd leave her there with a man neither of us knew.

"I guess I'm sure," she said.

So I had Paul sign the papers in front of me, and accordin' to what was written on 'em, that made 'em married. I gave one page to Paul, and filed the other at an attorney's office in Maynard later that day.

"Do you have any other sorts of tools I can use?"

"For what?"

"To bury a woman."

"Not a woman that big," Paul said.

"What difference does it make how big she is? You've either got some tools I can use or you don't."

He took another sip.

"Well then, I don't," he said.

About that time Phoebe came stompin' out of the sod shack. She stormed up to me and slapped my face as hard as it's ever been slapped.

"Whoa," Paul said. "That's one angry bitch."

Rose and Molly had followed Phoebe out the door and came to a stop behind her.

"Where's Monique?" I said, rubbbin' my jaw.

"Napping," Rose said.

To Phoebe I said, "What the hell's wrong with you?"

"You *shot* Molly?"

Molly held her hand up so I could see the little circle scar on the fleshy web between her thumb and forefinger.

"It's healed right nicely," I said. "Can't hardly tell."

Molly shrugged.

"What would possess you to shoot a woman in the hand?" Phoebe said. "She *paid* you to escort her all the way from Rolla and you *shot* her?"

"Well, she was wound pretty tight, and wouldn't follow my instructions," I said. "I feared she'd get us killed. And *would* have, had I not thought of a way to get her attention."

She looked at Molly, then back at me.

"Have you shot other women then?"

"A few."

Phoebe glared at me. "If that's the case I wonder how close you came to shooting *me*."

How close indeed, I thought.

With all of 'em standin' there, starin' at me, I chose that time to change the subject.

"We can't bury Scarlett here," I said.

"What?"

"We'll have to take her with us."

"What are you talking about? Take her where?"

"To Newton."

"That's insane."

"The ground around here is awful hard. Unless you got a pick and shovel in your bag I don't know about, we've got no tools to dig a hole with."

Phoebe was about to say somethin', but Paul spoke first. "I'll trade you a hole for that lean-to. I could make good use of that wood."

"You got a hole somewhere?"

"Nope. But I know where one is."

"Is it close?"

"It ain't far."

"Is it big enough and deep enough to bury Scarlett?"

He thought about it, then allowed, "We might have to fold her funny. But between the two of us we can probably wedge her in, if we kick her hard enough."

"*What?*" Phoebe said.

"I've got some rocks and remnant sod we can toss on top of her," Paul said.

It weren't the most elaborate way to send a fine woman like Scarlett to her final reward, but draggin' her behind a horse for six days weren't much better.

"It's unseemly," Phoebe said.

It *was* unseemly. Then again, we were on the prairie, where life and death is often unseemly. I waited a moment before lookin' at Phoebe.

"What do you think?" I said.

I knew Phoebe was angry, but I also knew she had a side to her that was so practical it had taken me by surprise the previous night when she considered usin' a child's grave for firewood. I didn't know how she might respond to this business of foldin' and kickin' Scarlett into a crazy sod-buster's hole. She was still upset with me about shootin' Molly, but this was a completely different subject, and I think she realized that among our group she was carryin' the banner for what was acceptable and what wasn't.

She said, "I don't see what other choice we have."

I looked at Paul. "Then let's do 'er."

I was glad Monique was nappin'. With any luck, Paul and I could get Scarlett buried before Monique found out about it. Then we could fetch her and the others, and speak some proper words over her grave.

I said, "Phoebe, will you and Rose go inside and keep an eye on Monique while we bury Scarlett?"

She narrowed her eyes at me and said, "I suppose if we don't, you'll shoot us."

CHAPTER 45

I TOOK NO pleasure in buryin' Scarlett.

Paul's hole had not been dug by someone anticipatin' the death of another. It was a natural hole that was more like a small cave, or animal's den. By lyin' on my stomach, I could get my head and shoulders far enough in it to see there were no skunks or fox or bobcats currently livin' there.

The front part was plenty wide, but it tapered toward the back, where it had a drop off that went deeper than I could see. If we could get at least part of her body into that drop off area, we could seal the front with enough rocks and sod to discourage even the most determined varmints from gettin' to her. I could only imagine the look on Monique or Phoebe's face later today if we were headin' to meet Shrug and came upon a raccoon or porcupine draggin' off one of Scarlett's body parts.

Gettin' Scarlett's body deep enough into the hole to properly bury her required doin' things to it that'll keep me out of heaven for six lifetimes. I could only hope the good Lord would accept part of the blame for creatin' such a large woman and allowin' her to die near such a small hole. I'm not the sort to criticize, but it seemed like bad plannin' to me, and I might've yelled that comment skyward, or worse ones, while actually doin' the deed.

In any case, after two hours of excruciatin' labor, it was done. I took two pieces of wood and some twine and made a cross and put it in the ground, knowin' what Paul was thinkin' as he watched me.

"Paul, no matter how much wood you might require to get through the next few winters, if this cross ain't here the next time I come through, I'm gonna shoot first and ask questions later."

"I won't use the wood."

"I have your word?"

"You do. But how can I keep someone else from usin' it? This ain't even my land!"

I shook my head. "I don't know, Paul. It ain't a fair burden to put on you, for sure. But someone's gotta be responsible. It's the least I can do for Scarlett. If you do the right thing and get shot anyway, maybe you can take some comfort knowin' God will sort it out later."

We walked Earl's horse back to Molly and Paul's, and had him drag the lean-to right up to the side of their hut. We removed it from his back, tied him to it, then gathered the women and brought 'em back to the grave site, where we spoke some solemn words. Then we sang three hymns, which was all the hymns I knew.

As we sang "Shall We Gather at the River," somethin' unusual happened. A red-tailed hawk flew over our heads, caught a puff of wind in its wings, and fanned them out to show the full majesty of its wingspan. Then it cut a wide arc in the sky, turned, and headed back toward us. A thing like that, so unexpected and beautiful, lifted our spirits and gave us hope that our dear Scarlett had been welcomed to the Pearly Gates with open arms. As the hawk passed low over our heads, he expelled a half-pound of bird shit that barely missed me, but hit Phoebe right between the eyes.

She looked up in the sky and shouted, "Fine!" She grabbed what shit she could from her face and flung it skyward, yellin', "Same to you!"

We all laughed, includin' Monique, despite her grief. On the way back to fetch our horses, Phoebe leaned in toward me and whispered, "Mr. Love? A word?"

We let the others go on ahead of us. While waitin' for 'em to get out of ear shot, I untied the bandana from my neck and wiped off as much bird shit as I could from Phoebe's hair. When we were alone, she said, "Have you ever been inside Paul and Molly's hut?"

"Nope. I try to keep outside them type a' houses."

"It is unlivable."

I nodded.

"Ungodly."

"Yes, ma'am."

"Unbelievable. Unhealthy. Unholy. Un—"

"I tried to tell you that."

"You did. But you didn't come close to capturing the living conditions. When Molly found out they could have the lean-to, it was as if she'd received an inheritance. How could she stay with a man who'd allow her to live like that?"

"Well, I've always said plains folk are a different breed. And to be fair, it ain't all Paul's fault they're livin' like that."

"What do you mean?"

"He's a hard luck man. Six years ago he had a yoke of oxen and a wagon that he traded for homestead rights to a nice piece of land in Maynard. He also had enough cash to make a down payment on two wagonloads of lumber, tools, and nails that he ordered from St. Joe, and financed the rest with a bank loan. With all that goin' for him, he placed his ad for a mail order bride, and Molly answered it."

"What happened to his house?"

"Well, lumber's a valuable commodity on the plains," I said. "Some thieves followed the shipment a few miles out of St. Joe, killed the drivers, and made off with the wagons, horses, and lumber."

"And what of the bank loan?"

"Paul couldn't pay it back. He lost his land and had to squat on this piece, and built a sod house so that when Molly showed up she'd have a place to live."

Her eyes clouded up. "That was a very noble thing for him to do," she said.

"That's why I said she may have been the one to get the bargain."

"On the other hand, she came here expecting to live in town, in a nice new home made of wood. The fact that she agreed to stay and live like this—" she gestured to the scrub area all around us—"speaks to her nobility as well."

"It does for a fact," I said. Then asked, "Is that what you wanted to talk about?"

"No."

I waited.

She said, "When we get to Mr. Pickett's so-called ranch..."

"Yes, ma'am?"

"If it turns out he's living in a sod house, or in circumstances so harsh that a load of dead tree limbs leaking with the residue of human suffering can make a grown woman cry for joy—do *not* allow me to stay there."

"Yes ma'am."

"I'd rather live in the cave where Wayne found me."

CHAPTER 46

SHRUG AND I had decided to meet up at Blackstrap Crick 'cause it was located a few miles from an old Indian trail that led all the way to Newton. It would've been too dangerous to travel just a few years earlier, but was relatively safe these days and offered the bonus of being mostly cleared.

When we approached the dried up banks of Blackstrap Crick, we found Shrug and the women watin' for us. Both groups ran toward each other, and when we collided, a lot of emotions passed back and forth, as well as stories about what had happened to each group. Gentry was pleased to see me, but after a quick hug and kiss, she ran off to hear Phoebe and Rose explain the details of what happened to Scarlett. That didn't bother me. Gentry had shared a parlor with Scarlett for more than two years, and except for Monique, had been her best friend.

The news about Scarlett brought down the spirits of the others, even as it lifted ours a bit to tell it. I suppose that's how grief works. By sharin' it with others, there's less for us to carry. Of course it was one more nail in little Hannah's heart. I wondered how much more her spirit could handle.

To me, the most amazin' part about reunitin' with the others was seein' what had become of Gentry's face. She had turned into the most beautiful woman I'd ever laid eyes on! Phoebe, especially, couldn't get over it.

"What on earth was in that poultice?" she asked Rose, shortly after we started the next part of our journey.

"A little of this and that," Rose said.

"Seriously, Rose, have you ever thought of patenting your formula and making it available back East? You could open a skin-care store. You'd make a fortune!"

"As many times as Gentry's already thanked me," Rose said, "I wouldn't have time to run a shop. Assuming the women of Philadelphia are half as grateful as she is."

"Too bad you've set your heart on bein' a rancher's wife in Newton, Kansas," I said. "Otherwise, Rose would probably finance your business venture."

"I will," Rose said. "If you decide not to marry your rancher fella. In fact, I have someone in mind who could help you run such a store."

"Maybe Mr. Pickett would like to become involved," Phoebe said.

"I wouldn't partner with a rancher," Rose said. "No offense."

"What do you have against ranchers?"

"I'd rather not say. You're about to be one, and I'd like us to stay friends."

"I'd like that, too," Phoebe said. She paused, then said, "Who is it you have in mind to help with the store?"

Rose said, "Let's wait until we see what happens between you and Mr. Pickett. No sense in worrying about a helper for a store that hasn't got an owner yet."

That night we made camp in my favorite spot in all of Kansas. Before the draught, this had been an oasis fit for a king. For miles around you'd find grass as high as a man's head in every direction, save for the twenty-foot-wide trail that led to this open area. Here, a river used to flow into a wide pool, and trickled into a small brook lined with cottonwood, elm, and hackberry trees. On this trip the grass around us lay dead and flat, and the water had dried up. Even so, it would be the prettiest camp we'd make before Dodge City, and it was in this place Phoebe asked me why Rose didn't care for ranchers.

"If Rose wanted you to know, she'd a' told you earlier," I said.

"Your loyalty to Rose runs deep," she said.

"I'm loyal to you, too."

"Not as loyal to me as to Rose, I suspect."

"Loyalty shouldn't have to be measured between two friends," I said. "Not if it runs both ways."

"What do you mean?"

"Rose and I are loyal to each other."

"So?"

"If she asked me somethin' about you that you didn't want revealed, I wouldn't answer, and she wouldn't press me to."

"You're probably a good friend to have, then," she said. "Apart from your Western ways."

"Apart from them," I said.

"In your opinion, would Rose make a good business partner?"

I laughed.

"What's so funny?"

"She proved her integrity by makin' the offer."

"I don't understand."

"It's her poultice and her money. What can you provide that she can't get from someone else back East who's already runnin' a successful skin care shop?"

She thought about that a minute. "You think she might steal my idea?"

I laughed again.

"What," she said.

"I'm not sure you're ready to settle down in Newton, Kansas."

"I've been thinking about it, that's all. There are precious few opportunities for women in the business world, so product is of paramount importance. And this poultice? The transformation in Gentry's appearance? Well, I've never seen anything like it! It's a product that could not possibly fail. And now that the idea's in my head, I don't know how to get it out."

"Well, you've got several days to ponder it."

It was dark. Soon the fireflies would be out. I didn't want to spoil the surprise for the others by talkin' about it in advance, but Shrug and I know this area as Firefly Heaven. In a half hour there'd be tens of thousands of fireflies puttin' on a show for us.

I heard a cough in the distance. Gentry, tryin' to get my attention. I aimed to be holdin' her in my arms when the light show started, and looked forward to seein' her reaction to one of nature's most glorious spectacles.

"Are you going to tell Rose we had this talk?" Phoebe said.

"Would you like me to?"

"No. Can I trust you not to tell her?"

"Of course."

"I wonder."

"Wonder what?"

"How we might be able to test this claim of loyalty you've professed to me," Phoebe said.

"How's Wayne?" I said.

Phoebe started to say "How should I–", but stopped abruptly. It was dark, and I couldn't see it, but I'm sure she blushed.

"I have no idea what you're referring to, I'm sure." Then she said, "But I'll trust you to keep your thoughts about it to yourself. As you said you'd do. Out of loyalty to me."

I looked up at the sky. "You need to be with Shrug."

"Why?"

"I'll let him tell you."

She followed my gaze.

"Is something bad about to happen?"

"No. Something beautiful."

CHAPTER 47

WATCHIN' THE SHOW at Firefly Heaven was like drinkin' whiskey, eatin' Gasconade perch, and watchin' nipple contests on the White River, meanin', they're all things Shrug and I have gone miles out of our way to enjoy. It seems like whenever I'm feelin' low, like I'd been feelin' lately on account of Scarlett's death, somethin' special will come along, like glorious fireflies, assertive nipples, or pan-fried Nade perch—and it puts me back in mind that life is good.

Speakin' of assertive nipples, I had good cause durin' the firefly show to wonder how I could've supposed Leah or anyone else on God's earth could've bested Gentry in such a contest. Then again, I was no longer an impartial judge.

Firefly Heaven was only five days from Newton, Kansas, Phoebe's droppin' off point. The trail was well-defined, and there weren't any surprises along it. While Shrug scouted out far ahead, the women and I quickly settled into the daily routine that defines wagon travel: up at daybreak, cook breakfast, saddle the horses, yoke the oxen, break the camp, ride the trail, break for lunch and necessaries, stop at seven, make the camp, tend to the livestock, cook dinner, fuck Gentry...

And so it went.

On the fifth night, around eight-thirty, Phoebe asked if we could chat. I figured she was goin' to talk about Shrug, and explain why she'd been ignorin' him more and more with each passin' evenin'. I already knew why: she was about to meet the man she'd agreed to marry, and her relationship with Shrug had to come to an end in order to give Mr. Pickett his due. It was better to put her feelin's toward Shrug behind her, at least until she'd had a chance to decide about Pickett.

But what she wanted to talk about had nothin' to do with Shrug.

What she said was, "Do you think I'd be a good business woman?"

I said, "Can't get it out of your mind, can you?"

"It tugs at me," she said. "What Rose did for Gentry's face, why, it's nothing short of a miracle! It's something every woman would want. And there are thousands upon thousands of women in Philadelphia who would pay a small fortune for it. Especially if we claimed there was a limited supply. It would build up enormous demand."

"I *know* you'd be a great business woman."

"What makes you so sure?"

"Two things. First, you can't get it out of your system. And second, you're the bravest woman I've ever known."

"Excuse me?"

"It's true."

"Me?"

"Sit down," I said. She did. I said, "You remember the first day we met?"

"Of course."

"I was ridin' Major, followin' the stones Shrug had placed, and suddenly I saw a woman's footprint."

"So?"

"If you could've seen the look on my face you'd know how unique an event that was."

"I'd been foolish. I took an unnecessary chance. I could have been killed."

"It was the single bravest act I ever witnessed," I said. "A woman travelin' alone, on foot, through the Ozarks, with nothin' but fancy clothes and a sack full of coffee..."

"You've always been a fool for my coffee!" she said, smilin'.

I chuckled. "You're braver than I am."

"How so?"

"I've often thought of buyin' a business."

"Really? What type of business?"

"There's a little saloon and card emporium in Dodge City called *The Lucky Spur*, that's owned by a friend of mine. It's where I spend a lot of time after deliverin' the women to the brothels. Every time I go there, my friend Hank tells me I should settle down and buy the place."

"Why don't you?"

"Guess I don't have your grit. Or your head for business."

"Well, if it's an established business..."

"It is."

"Then the existing employees could run the place. All you'd have to do is make sure they aren't stealing from you."

"Who'd dare steal from me?"

"Exactly. And don't they have someone standing guard every night?"

"They do."

"You could save money by taking that job yourself. You'd be in the place you enjoy, doing work you're good at, and you'd own the business. I should think you'd have a very successful enterprise, especially with the draw."

"The what?"

"The attraction."

"Which is what?"

"You, silly! You're a famous gunman, are you not?"

"I'm not unknown, I suppose."

"I'm sure droves of people in Dodge City would frequent a saloon and card emporium if they knew it was owned by the famous gunman Emmett Love. Especially if they could actually see you standing guard, and possibly make your acquaintance."

We let that thought hang in the air awhile. Then I said, "Well, anyway, we were talkin' about your skin care shop in Philadelphia."

"Alas, tomorrow I'm to meet my betrothed."

"As it currently stands."

"I'd be a fool to come all this way and not even meet the man."

I didn't say anything.

"Wouldn't I?" she said.

CHAPTER 48

IT WAS TWO in the afternoon when we rolled into Newton. After parkin' the oxen and wagons at the livery stable, me and Phoebe watered the horses and tied her huge carpetbag to Earl's horse. She and the women said their tearful goodbyes, then Rose led them down the street to the Adelaide Hotel, where we planned to spend the night, get a bath, and have a nice dinner together. Gentry and I planned to share a room, and the girls would do the same, with Monique, Hester and Leah in one room and Mary and Emma in another. With great enthusiasm Rose offered to share her room with Hannah, but the hapless child seemed not to care who she bunked with. I had the feeling she would have shown no expression had we bunked her with a mule.

Phoebe and me climbed on our horses and started walkin' 'em through town.

"Where's Wayne?" she said.

"He's probably staked out a spot on Pickett's ranch where he can keep an eye on things."

She smiled. "He's a good friend."

"There ain't no better friend in the world than Shrug," I said.

"How long will he stay there?"

"That I don't know. But if you were to scream his name tonight in an urgent way, you'd best duck, because rocks are gonna fly!"

She laughed.

"I finally understand it," she said.

"What's that?"

"The relationship you and Wayne have."

"Well good for you, because I don't have a clue about it. Just seems to work, is all I know."

"Whoa," I said. Major stopped, and Phoebe jerked Earl's horse to a stop as well.

"I don't think you'll have to worry about livin' in a sod house," I said.

"Why not?"

I pointed to all four corners of Main Street, where it intersected with First. Where the signs said PICKETT'S FEED STORE, PICKETT'S SALOON, PICKETT'S LUMBER & HARDWARE, and THE PICKETT DAILY NEWS.

"My word!" Phoebe said.

"My word, indeed," I said. We paused a moment, watching the activity around her future husband's businesses, then headed out of town, toward Pickett's ranch.

Turns out Mr. Pickett was a very prominent businessman. Turns out he had a wonderful spread, more than five hundred acres, with a beautiful two-story wood and brick house. Turns out the house had a wide veranda, complete with a handrail that wrapped elegantly around the front of the house, and rockin' chairs where people could drink lemonade while enjoyin' friendly conversation. I know, because it was on that very porch that Phoebe and I sat with Mr. Pickett and shared a lovely afternoon.

To my great happiness, he appeared to be a kind and charming man. He positively doted on Phoebe from the moment she arrived, and he insisted on showing us the house, grounds, and stables, and introduced us to his servants and his French cook and his ranch hands, and...

And that's where I got a funny feelin'.

Because some of the ranch hands looked a lot like gunmen.

CHAPTER 49

AFTER THE TOUR I told Mr. Pickett I wanted to talk to Phoebe in private. He took her hand, kissed it and said, "I know what he's going to ask you, and I hope you'll say yes. But if not, there'll be no hard feelings, and I'll make sure you're escorted safely back to Philadelphia in the most comfortable manner possible, at my complete expense."

She dipped her knee in a way that was probably cultured, and then she tittered, or whatever they call it when a woman pretends to be impressed by some high-falutin', hand-kissin' mucky muck.

Or maybe she was impressed.

"Sod house, indeed!" she said when we were alone on the porch. I mean, veranda.

"It's a far cry from Paul and Molly's," I said.

"Poor Molly," she said. "It doesn't seem fair, does it?"

"I think those ranch hands are hired gunmen," I said.

"What? Oh, pooh."

"I'm serious, Phoebe. There's more here than meets the eye."

"Please! Keep your voice down!" She took my arm and pulled me off the porch, out into the open, making certain no one could hear our conversation.

"So what if they're hired gunmen," she said.

"*What?*"

"If you owned all this, wouldn't you want to surround yourself with men who can keep trouble out?"

"I don't know. Maybe. But if I did, I wouldn't introduce them as ranch hands."

"He was probably being respectful to the gunmen," she said. "And anyway, no one has confirmed that they are, indeed, gunmen. So far it's just you making the assumption."

"How many gunfights you been in?" I said.

She gave me a look. "How many do you think?"

"I reckon I know gunslingers when I see 'em," I said.

"Oh, Emmett. You and Shrug, my noble knights. Always so quick to defend me. Even when there's no danger."

"I'm not sayin' it ain't a grand way to live. And I ain't sayin' you shouldn't marry the man."

"Then what *are* you saying, Emmett?"

"I think you should put him off."

"What? He's expecting an answer. It would be terribly rude to put him off at this point."

"Just until I have time to ask around."

"No."

"No?"

"I want to marry him, Emmett. The man is a prize. The type of prize a woman can only dream of! Not only is he the most charming man I've ever met, he's also the most humble."

"Humble?"

"What would *you* call it? He never once mentioned the true size of his estate, or the businesses he owns, or the number of cattle he has, or even the quality of his home."

"He told us he started small and kept workin' hard."

"I should think that would have impressed you."

"Normally it would. But you don't build somethin' this size by startin' small and workin' hard."

"Now you sound jealous."

I nodded. "I can see why you might think that. And maybe I am, and don't know it. But that don't make me wrong."

"I'm willing to take my chances that Mr. Pickett is for real."

"What about the poultice business with Rose?"

"What about it?"

"Will you be able to get it out of your head?"

She paused. "No, probably not. But I'll be so busy here, arranging parties and teas, and making my husband happy, I doubt I'll have much time to dwell on it."

I eyed her carefully as I said, "What about Shrug?"

She sighed. "Dear Shrug. Do you see him? Is he out there somewhere right now, watching us?"

I noticed it was the first time she'd called him Shrug, which I took as a bad sign. "Shrug ain't the type of person you can see, less he wants to be seen. But he's out there, you can bet. And I s'pect he don't like the look a' them fellers any more than I do."

"Wayne is a dear friend. As you are, Emmett. And I can't tell you how happy I am to have met you both." She sighed again, for emphasis. "But I'm ready to begin the next phase of my life. So if you don't mind, let's go tell Mr. Pickett that I'd be thrilled to marry him, and I'll have him pay your fee before I sign the papers."

"My what?"

"Your twenty dollars. In gold, just as we agreed. Wait," she said. "You seem offended."

"I *am* offended."

"But why?"

"Well, I don't rightly know."

"We had an agreement, did we not?"

"I reckon we did. But–"

"But what?"

I shook my head. "I don't know. It just...*seems* different somehow."

"You've accepted money from the others."

"I have."

"Even Gentry."

"Yes."

"It would be ridiculous not to accept my husband's money. It would, in fact, be improper."

I sighed. I really didn't know why her offerin' to pay me stuck so thick in my craw. Made no sense. And anyway, twenty dollars was a pitiful sum compared to what others would have charged to bring a tenderfoot four hundred miles. Of course, others wouldn't have made her carry a lean-to all those miles, or put her in a position to get hit in the head with hawk shit.

"Okay," I said. "Let's give him the good news. But don't sign anythin' tonight."

"Emmett, you needn't worry about me signing any papers. This is nothing like Molly and Paul or the others you've brought together. Mr. Pickett and I will be married in a church or here at the ranch, by a real preacher. There will be guests, and music, and flowers, and who knows what else."

It was the 'what else' that bothered me. But I said, "I'll accept your decision and say no more about it, except this: tomorrow mornin', instead of leavin' at dawn, I'll wait until eight o'clock to hitch the team. That'll give you the whole night to think on it. If you change your mind, just get your bag and start walkin', and Shrug'll be at your side before you get a hundred yards."

"I'm not going to change my mind, Emmett. And even if I did, Mr. Pickett has graciously agreed to make sure I'm returned to Philadelphia safely, in an elegant way."

I was afraid Mr. Pickett's intentions of returnin' her might involve havin' his gunmen shoot her for rejectin' him. I looked her dead in the eye. "Phoebe, if for any reason you decide not to marry the man, do *not* accept his offer to send you back."

"Why not?"

"Trust me on this one thing."

"Why should I?"

"Because I'm right. And because—"

"Yes?"

"I'm loyal."

She sighed a big, frustrated sigh.

"Fine," she said. "What difference does it make? I'm not going to change my mind in the first place."

"I'll wait at the livery tomorrow mornin'," I said.

"I know. Until eight. Thank you, Emmett, that's really very gallant of you. I know how you like to be on the trail first thing in the morning."

I looked into her eyes, and she looked back. She'd made up her mind.

"Okay," I said. "That's all I've got to say."

She kissed my cheek and said, "Thank you, Emmett. Now let's get this done!"

CHAPTER 50

WE HAD A fine dinner and a wonderful time at the Hotel Adelaide's restaurant. As a group, we hadn't laughed since Scarlett's passin'. But on this night, everyone seemed happy. Rose, often considered aloof, was openly friendly, and to my surprise, funny. Even Monique had a good time! Of course, little Hannah's expression never changed. But who could blame her? She probably expected the roof to cave in on us. As the laughter got louder, a couple of young cowboys approached our table and asked if any of the ladies might care to dance.

"You hear any music?" Mary said, teasin' him along. "I don't hear any."

One of the cowboys said, "In a few minutes there'll be plenty of dance music down the street at Pickett's."

Out of instinct, I put my hand in my pocket and felt the twenty dollar gold piece Pickett had given as payment in full for Phoebe's transport.

"Can we go, Emmett?" Leah asked.

Mary snorted, "Who is he, your *father*? Of *course* we can go!"

Rose said, "I'm going to take Hannah on up to bed. Have fun, ladies!" She and Hannah got up to leave. "Goodnight, Emmett. Thank you for dinner."

"My pleasure. Goodnight, Rose, goodnight, Hannah."

Gentry also bid them good night.

Rose told the women to be careful.

"It's these cowboys that need to be careful," Emma said, laughin'.

"We leave at eight," I said. "Don't forget."

"Yes, Daddy," Leah said.

"Goodnight, Daddy," Emma said.

"Don't wait up for us," Hester added.

"Will you spank me, Daddy?" Mary said, tossin' her hair. She shook her ass at me, then saw Gentry's look and said, "No offense, Gentry. Maybe these young gentlemen will let me shake it at them."

The cowboys laughed and nudged each other. They knew a sure thing when they saw it.

One by one they left, until it was just me and Gentry sittin' at the table, waitin' to pay the bill. Gentry said, "Will you take me to Pickett's?"

"I reckon we should see what all the fuss is about, maybe have a drink."

Gentry's gorgeous, normal-colored face lit up. "Yay!" she said.

I said, "Since the music ain't started yet, there's somethin' I'd really like to do first, if you don't mind."

"Of course, Emmett. What do you have in mind?"

"I'd like to take you for a little stroll through town."

"A stroll?"

"If you don't mind."

"You'd escort me? Like the town men do with real ladies?"

"Of course."

Her smile started small and kept growin' until it seemed to take up her whole face. It was the type of smile a man would work all day just to come home to. Gentry started to speak, but choked on her words. She dipped her head for a second. When she looked back up at me I could see tears wellin' up in her eyes. But she was still smilin'. She swallowed, and said, "I'd be honored."

I paid the bill and Gentry and I headed down Main Street, arm-in-arm. She cozied up to me and purred, "This is real nice, Emmett. You're making me feel quite special."

"I'm proud to be with you, Gentry."

We strolled to the end of town on one side of the street and started headin' back on the other. Gentry said, "I miss Scarlett."

I said, "I know you do."

She said, "I hate to let anyone go. I even miss Phoebe! Can you just imagine?"

"Phoebe grows on people, over time."

"Like I do?"

I smiled. "I liked you from the very first day."

"Out of everyone I ever met," Gentry said, "I'm gonna miss you the most."

"Well, I was already plannin' to hang around Dodge for two weeks. But I'll stay longer if you like, at least 'til you get settled in."

She stopped and gave me a kiss. "You're a good man, Emmett Love."

"You make me better than I am."

Across the street, on the boardwalk, a boy rolled a spokeless wagon wheel with a stick, and got it goin' so fast he nearly ran into the portly gentleman who was lockin' up the dry goods store. "Watch where you're goin', you hellion!" he shouted.

The boy tipped his hat to the man and said, "Sorry, Mr. Grant."

We watched Mr. Grant turn the corner, and we resumed our stroll. A moment later we heard the sound of glass shatterin' in the dry goods store.

"Boys," Gentry said.

"Some things never change," I said.

"You think Phoebe and her fella will stroll the town on Sundays?" she said.

"I s'pect they will." Then I said, "Did I do the right thing by Phoebe today?"

"You said her mind was made up."

"It was."

"And she's a grown woman."

"She is. And a strong one at that."

"And they exchanged a lot of letters over time. So she knows him pretty well."

I hadn't thought about that.

"True," I said. "Of course, in all them letters he never mentioned his wealth, nor his rise to prominence."

"Prominence? That's a mighty big word for a gunslinger! You keep speaking big words at me, who knows *what* might happen later tonight!"

I smiled. "I look forward to it. Indubitably."

"Woooh!" Gentry giggled, pretendin' to be charmed.

Was Pickett, as Phoebe claimed, just a humble man? Or was he up to somethin'? And if so, what could it be? Phoebe was a wonderful woman, and a right pretty one at that. But...

"Why Phoebe?" I said.

"What do you mean?"

"Why would a man like Pickett send off for a mail-order bride? If he's as big a catch as Phoebe claims, he ought to have his pick of women from here to Wichita. You don't suppose the women around here know enough about him to stay away, do you?"

"What's he look like?"

"He ain't the most handsome feller I've seen. But he ain't ugly, neither. And what he lacks in looks, he makes up for in charm."

"He's recently wealthy?"

"Pretty recent," I said. "Last few years, I believe."

"Worked his way up from nothin'?"

"That's what he told us."

"Political aspirations?"

"What's that mean?"

"Did he say anything about runnin' for Mayor? Or Governor?"

"He can't run for Governor, Gentry."

"Why not?"

"Kansas ain't even a state yet."

"But everyone's talkin' about it. They're sayin' January, which is not but three months away."

"True," I said. "But what's that got to do with Phoebe?"

"It's just a theory," Gentry said.

"I'd like to hear it."

"Self-made man, small town background, startin' to rise in the world of business. Could it be he's tryin' to buy some class?"

"What do you mean?"

"Maybe he's plannin' to jump into the governor's race, and wants a beautiful, sophisticated Eastern wife on his arm to help him work his way into high society."

"If we're that close to statehood, it might be too late for that."

"But not too late to start makin' contacts for the next election."

"You're a lot smarter than me," I said.

"Smart enough to know a good man when I see one," she said.

"Even when he's old enough to be your father?"

She smiled. "Especially then."

"Why's that?"

"Young men don't appreciate a diamond in the rough like me."

"They will now."

"What, because of my new face? Where were they when I was ugly?"

"You were never ugly. Not even close."

"See? That's what I mean by appreciation. Means a lot to an impressionable young sprite like myself."

"You ain't impressionable, neither," I said. "For all my age and experience, you've taught me some things under the blanket I'd never known."

Gentry laughed out loud. "If blanket learnin' suits you, I've got plenty left to teach."

"Oh Lordy," I said.

Newton was a small town, and we'd strolled it both ways. As we were about to turn the corner and head to Pickett's, we found ourselves standin' in front of the sheriff's office. I said, "Let's go in a minute. I want to ask him somethin'."

CHAPTER 51

"SALT OF THE earth," the sheriff said. "Never met a better man than Hiram Pickett."

"How did he acquire his wealth?" I said.

"He just started small and kept workin'," he said.

"Sounds like a campaign slogan," Gentry said.

Sheriff Kilbourne had been admirin' Gentry's figure since we entered his office. When she spoke, he got a chance to admire her face.

"Christ A'mighty!" he said. "Heaven done sent us an angel! What's your name, sugar?"

"Emmett's Woman," she said, sweet as pie.

Kilbourne looked at me with different eyes. "And you must be Emmett."

"I am."

Kilbourne removed his hat and placed it on the table. He ran his hand over his head. "No offense, but I wouldn't a' put you two together." He sighed. "You're a lucky man, Emmett, 'cause she's about the prettiest thing I ever seen. I don't even have to ask if she's from around here. But I hope you folks ain't plannin' to leave anytime soon, because the whole town will look better with her in it."

"Thanks, but I'm spoken for," she said.

Sheriff Kilbourne had short hair and a wide face that needed shavin'. His eyes were closer together than most folks, and he was sittin' on a hard-backed chair at his desk with his right leg stretched out on a smaller footstool. He noticed me lookin' at his leg.

"Sorry for not standin' up to greet you proper," he said. He pointed to his foot. "Gout."

"Foot or toe?"

"Both."

"That's gotta hurt."

He smiled. "Ben Franklin once said that a man can't be in love and have a toothache at the same time. But Franklin never laid eyes on Gentry here," he said.

Gentry ignored the flirt. She said, "You think Hiram Pickett might run for governor some day?"

"We don't need a State Governor yet," he said. "And Territorial Governor's an appointed position."

"Kansas already has one, don't they?" I said.

"They come and go pretty fast. No one's been able to hold the position very long."

"Maybe Pickett will change all that," I said.

"Well, he'd make a good one," Kilbourne said.

I nodded, and we started to leave. Kilbourne said, "When you do decide to leave, which way are you headed?"

"St. Joe," I lied.

"You ever been there before?"

"I have."

"Ever stay at the Patee House?"

The Patee House was the nicest hotel west of the Mississippi. Had a ballroom and barbershop.

"A bit fancy for my budget," I said.

CHAPTER 52

AT EIGHT THE next mornin' none of the women were happy except Gentry. Mary, Leah, Hester and Emma complained about the way they felt after a long night of heavy drinkin' and randy behavior. They claimed to have been grievously over-served. As Mary put it, "I feel like a mouse army is crawlin' through my innards." Monique wasn't speakin' at all. Hannah was sober as a judge, and Rose was gettin' fidgety.

"It's eight," she said. "Guess I'm not going to own a skin care shop in Philadelphia."

"We should give her a little more time," I said.

"The wagons are ready to roll, Emmett. And Phoebe's got Shrug there, keeping an eye on her. If she wants to leave, he'll bring her to us.

"Just a few more minutes."

Rose sighed, and kept a frown on her face, but said nothin' more about it.

A half hour later, the whores were sprawled out on the hay, sleepin'. Someone was snorin' like a pregnant sow, but I couldn't tell who, and nor did I care. The lot of 'em looked like death warmed over, 'cept for Monique, who always looked high style and refined.

Rose caught Gentry's eye and nodded in my direction. Gentry said, "She's not comin', Emmett. Let her be. She's happy."

"You're probably right," I said. But I had a feelin' about it I couldn't shake.

At nine Rose said, "Emmett, we're burning daylight. If you want to stay awhile longer, at least let me get started. You and Gentry can take the horses and catch up when it suits you."

"Fair enough," I said. "I won't be much longer, but you're right. There's no need to hold everyone else up."

"Finally!" she said. "Let's go, ladies, before he changes his mind!"

I looked at Gentry. "You want to go with 'em?"

"My place is with you, Emmett. Long as you want me."

"Gentry, you're a beautiful, young woman..."

"Emmett, don't even start. We've been through this before. You're not too old for me. You're just right."

We watched Rose roust up the half-drunk whores and get 'em in the wagons. Only Monique was sober enough to drive the second wagon, though she had little experience. Rose spoke to her in French, and Monique reluctantly took her place on the seat of the second wagon.

"I told her if she keeps the oxen close behind my wagon, she won't have any problems," Rose explained.

"Good advice," I said. "Thanks, Rose."

She climbed in the lead wagon, lifted the reins and snapped them down, while callin' "Heeyuh!" The oxen strained forward slowly, waitin' for the wheels to turn. Soon they were movin' down the street. Rose lifted her right hand high above her head and waved at us without turnin' around.

"She was gettin' riled with you," Gentry said.

"She don't like to be kept waitin'."

"What woman does?" Gentry said. Then she said, "You wanna go for another stroll? Get some more store-bought coffee?"

"I had more coffee this mornin' than I know what to do with."

She kissed my cheek. "I know you're partial to Phoebe's coffee, but I'll work on mine. It won't be the same, but over time I'll get pretty good at it. You'll see."

"We're too far apart, Gentry. I'll be old and sick some day and you'll still be in your prime."

"Do all your excuses amount to bein' afraid I'm gonna leave you someday?"

"I suppose."

"Emmett, no offense, but that's the dumbest thing you could possibly worry about."

"Why's that?"

"You're afraid I'm gonna leave someday. What, two years? Five years? Ten?"

"I don't know when. I just know it's gonna happen."

"And because of that, you're willin' to give up all the special times we could have in the meantime?"

"Well–"

"Emmett Love, what the hell have you got goin' in your life that would be more enjoyable if you were doin' it without me?"

She had a point.

"Look," she said. "I don't know how I'll feel in ten years, but I know I love bein' with you right now, and will for a long time. And I'm not askin' you to marry me or make me a proper woman. But I'll damn sure ride with you on these crazy ass, no-profit trips, and there's a lot I can do to help. I can cook some, and pack a bag. I can build a fire. I'm a good rider. I can saddle horses and help yoke oxen. I can hold my water for long periods of time and handle bad weather without complaint. I wake up easy and don't drink to excess. I'm fun and perky and have a sunny disposition. I can bring in more than my share of cash, too, by whorin' in the towns we pass along the way."

"No woman of mine is gonna whore," I said, defiantly.

Gentry smiled.

"I'm good with that," she said.

"S'cuse me," the stable boy said. "Comin' through."

We'd been standin' inside one of the empty stalls that faced the street. The stall belonged to a customer's horse the kid had been exercisin' and groomin' since we arrived. But now it was time for him to reclaim the space.

Gentry looked at me. "It's ten o'clock. You ready to saddle up, cowboy?"

I looked up and down the street.

"I reckon she ain't comin'," I said.

"Time to move on with our lives," Gentry said. "That's what Phoebe did, and it's the natural order of things."

CHAPTER 53

IT ONLY TOOK twenty minutes to catch up to the others. When we did, Gentry and I rode out in front, wavin' as we passed. I kept lookin' ahead, from side to side.

"Are you lookin' for stones?" Gentry said.

"It's a habit," I said. "Shrug ain't likely to be out ahead of us yet."

"You think he's still at Pickett's?"

"I do."

"You think he's in love with Phoebe?"

I did, but didn't say anythin'. Goes back to that loyalty idea me and Phoebe spoke about the other night.

"I think he loves her deeply," she said.

The trail to Dodge City was well-tramped and wide. There was decent water here, and the grass was in better shape than where we'd been.

"How far to Dodge City?"

"Oxen move slowly," I said.

"What does that mean time-wise?"

"Four days."

"So why didn't you just say that?"

I shrugged. "I'm a cowboy. We're supposed to talk like that."

We rode an extra hour to make up for the time I wasted that mornin', waitin' on Phoebe. Then we camped on Cow Creek, on the northeast side of the Arkansas River.

"There's a lot of salt in this area," Rose said, sniffin' the air.

"You always say that," I reminded her.

"This time I was telling Hannah," she said.

I smiled and waved at Hannah, and waited to see if she'd wave back. No smile, no wave. If I didn't know better, I'd swear she was blind.

Cow Creek was part of the Sand Prairie. It weren't nothin' special to look at, but we weren't fussy. I managed to shoot a jackrabbit that Rose was more than happy to clean and add to the cook pot. Gentry insisted on helpin' her, and Rose was kind enough to let her, though it slowed her down considerable.

After dinner, Gentry and I took up our usual position between my two large blankets, away from the others. The nights were turnin' frosty, so she'd brought an extra blanket for later, when the actual sleepin' would take place.

After enjoyin' a poke, I said, "I been thinkin' about settlin' down."

She sat up so fast the blanket didn't have time to catch up.

Enjoyin' the view, I said, "You're a fine figure of a gal, Gentry."

"Never mind that," she said, wrappin' her spare blanket around her. "What type of settlin' down are you talkin' about?"

I told her about my idea for buyin' *The Lucky Spur* in Dodge City.

"Really Emmett? Because that would be wonderful!"

"Right now it's just a thought flittin' around in my head."

"Well, if you decide to do it, I'd love to be a part of it. I could help you in a hundred different ways."

Then she proceeded to list them, one at a time, to the point I wished I hadn't brought it up. Somewhere around her fifteenth idea of how to help me run *The Lucky Spur*, I kissed her on the mouth, and kept kissin' 'til she hushed talkin'.

The next day was like the first, except that the whores were gettin' excited about the trip finally comin' to a close. They were eager to rise, short to break, and pushed me to travel longer than I cared to. As a group, they put me in mind of a cold mule that knows he's gettin' closer to a warm barn.

There was still no sign of Shrug, and I was surprised he'd waited so long to make sure Phoebe was safe and happy with Pickett. I kept lookin' for him anyway, knowin' he'd turn up eventually. I figured he was in love with Phoebe, but I knew he wouldn't hang around the ranch the rest of her life. I did believe he'd stop by Pickett's place from time to time to spy on her and see if she was bein' treated okay. I hoped so, for Pickett's sake, because I wouldn't want to be on Shrug's bad side.

I finally accepted the fact that Phoebe made a decision that was best for her. I figured her to be happier with the lifestyle than the man, but those sorts of things like parties and teas and polite conversations and community status were important to women like Phoebe, and I was happy for her. While Phoebe and I weren't a perfect match for each other as friends, we were a decent one, and I'd grown close to her over the course of the trip. She had many more good qualities than bad, and now that she was gone, I could hardly remember any of the bad. I took a minute to think about how, in any other setting, she and I would have never had an occasion to meet, or speak to each other, and certainly wouldn't have forged a friendship. But I liked her, and knew I always would. I'd probably stop in to check on her myself, from time to time.

These thoughts of becomin' friends with Phoebe and then sayin' goodbye put me in mind of Scarlett and Monique, and how they shared a special carin' for each other. Monique was devastated, and feelin' lost right now, but I bet she cherished the time they *had* spent together. And what of little somber-faced Hannah? It was clear that Rose was growin' fond of the doleful child, and that was good news for both of 'em. I wouldn't be surprised if Rose decided to take her back to Springfield with her. Who knows what type of lady Hannah might grow up to be with a woman like Rose lookin' after her?

Hannah was always worried about what might happen to destroy her world. And with good cause. But wouldn't it be better for her to enjoy her time with Rose instead of worryin' when it might end?

It's like what Gentry had said. I wondered how many people avoided the *deepness* of love 'cause there weren't no guarantees on the *length* of it.

We made camp that night on the Coon Creek battlefield, where soldiers used breechloadin' rifles against Indians for the first time.

After dinner and a poke, Gentry said, "Any more thoughts on *The Lucky Spur*?"

"I didn't really think on it much today," I said. "What about you?"

"I only care if you're happy, Emmett. My happiness don't depend on what you *do*, but how you *feel*."

"You're a helluva woman," Gentry.

"So I'm a woman now, huh?"

"You're *all* woman."

"Glad you noticed. Now don't forget it!"

CHAPTER 54

IT WAS THE third night out of Newton, and we camped late, on a stretch of land that felt good under my feet. There was deep soil here, the type that produces the most abundant crops. The air had a clean scent to it, and there was plenty of wildlife to be seen and heard.

Bein' the last night we'd all be together, I broke out the bottle of bourbon I'd brought all the way from Rolla. I'd bought two, given one to Shrug the first day out when he'd strung a line of perch for me near the Gasconade River—and figured it was time to put this second one to good use.

We ate and sang and danced 'til the whiskey was gone, and then sang and danced some more. Bein' the only man, I got a lot of attention from the womenfolk, and yet all through the evenin', no matter how wild the dancin' got, Gentry kept givin' me love looks that warmed my heart. That night, when we bedded down, I said, "Gentry."

"Yes, Emmett?"

"I love you."

She didn't respond.

"Did you hear me?" I said.

"Yes."

"Well aren't you gonna say nothin'?"

"I'm sayin' it with my heart. Can't you hear me?"

"Say it with your voice so I'll be sure to know."

"I love you truly, Emmett. And I always will."

"Sayin' it brings an obligation."

"Oh, Emmett."

"What?"

"You're not gonna ruin the moment by gettin' all serious, are you?"

Was I?

No.

"I've made a decision," I said.

She waited.

"I'm gonna buy *The Lucky Spur*."

"Why, that's great news, Emmett!"

"And I want you to live with me."

"A' course I will!"

"And I want you to stop whorin'."

"You'll save a heap of money right there!"

"How's that?"

"Because you'll be gettin' it for free, silly."

I smiled. "It gets better and better, don't it!"

"It does," she said.

"There's one more thing."

"What's that?"

"I've decided that whatever time you'll give me, I'm gonna take."

"And?"

"And I'll be happy."

"And?"

"And I won't worry about when it might end."

"That's all I'll ever ask," she said.

CHAPTER 55

THE NEXT MORNIN', just before sunup, I smelled the unmistakable aroma of Rose's famous fried biscuits and ham. Me and Gentry had set our blankets a ways from camp, so I had to holler to make myself heard.

"What time is it?" I shouted.

"Nearly five," Rose shouted back.

"Smells great," I hollered. "But ain't it awful early?"

"We've got company."

I looked around.

"Where?"

"You'll see. Put your pants on."

A minute later I heard the sound a wood warbler makes, far in the distance. I whistled back.

"What's up?" Gentry said, yawnin'.

"Shrug's comin'."

"Finally!" Gentry said.

I wasn't surprised Shrug was joinin' us, though I'd expected him sooner. But I *was* surprised to see he'd brought Phoebe Thayer with him.

No one wanted to do anythin' but eat and hear their story. And since I'd never known Shrug to speak, it was all on Phoebe to tell it.

CHAPTER 56

"MR. PICKETT WAS a complete gentleman," Phoebe said, "from start to finish. He's a charming man, extremely wealthy, and has high political aspirations."

Gentry nudged me, smiled, and mouthed the words "Told you!"

Mary said, "Wait—before you say anything else—is Mr. Pickett available?"

Phoebe laughed. "He's all yours, Mary."

"If he was all those things," I said, "why aren't you still with him?"

"Because he's dishonest. Or was, at least."

"Dishonest how?"

"You know his lumber business?"

I nodded.

"He claims his businesses are completely legitimate now, but admits he hired some gunmen to rob wagonloads of lumber in Kansas, Missouri, and Nebraska."

I thought about Molly and Paul, and how the robbers had killed the drivers and made off with Paul's life savings. "How did you come by that knowledge?"

"My second day there, Wayne led me to a small gully where he'd found a dozen old wagons covered with canvas. On the side of the wagons I saw lettering that identified them as belonging to various lumber yards in several states."

"Were any of 'em from St. Joe?"

"Six."

"Were two of 'em Paul's?"

"I don't think so, Emmett, but I can't say for sure."

"What did you do?"

"I confronted Mr. Pickett."

"And he admitted it?"

"Not right away."

"How'd you get him to talk?"

Phoebe looked at Shrug. "Wayne helped."

Shrug grinned.

"What did he do?"

"He set the barn on fire. When the ranch hands ran to put it out, he knocked them unconscious with rocks and tied them up."

"There must've been ten men!" I said. "How could one man tie up ten?"

"Every time one of them started to come to, Wayne hit him over the head and kept tying. When Mr. Pickett came outside to help, Wayne dragged him back into the house."

"And he confessed?"

"Eventually."

"Aren't you afraid he's gonna come after you and try to kill you?"

"No."

"Why not?"

"Because I sold him my silence."

"How?" Mary said.

"He opened his safe and gave me a substantial sum of money."

"Enough to get back East?"

"More."

"Enough to open your skin care shop?" I said.

"It would be," she said. "But I have a better use for it. I'm giving the bulk of it to Paul Snow, so he can build a proper house for his nagging, gunshot wife. There should be enough left over for us to order a proper headstone for Scarlett's grave."

Rose had been quietly translatin' everythin' to Monique from the moment Phoebe started talkin'. When she got to that part, Monique burst into tears.

"You were happy livin' on Pickett's ranch," I said.

"I was."

"And he was a perfect gentleman."

"Yes."

"Do you believe he's honest now?"

"I do. And if his men were responsible for the killing, I don't think he knew it. He seemed devastated about it and said none of the local papers reported any deaths in connection with the wagons he stole."

"It'd be a big coincidence if he didn't heist Paul's shipment."

"I agree."

"It seemed like a perfect life for you," I said.

"It did. But it was a life built on the suffering of others. I tried to overlook it, tried to justify it was all in the past. But in the end, I couldn't do it. Also, there was something else."

"What's that?" Mary said.

"I couldn't get the idea out of my head. Starting my own business with Rose, in Philadelphia." Phoebe looked at Rose. "Is your generous offer still on the table?"

"It is," Rose said.

"Excellent!"

Then Phoebe said, "When will you introduce me to the person you said would help me get started?"

"You already know her," Rose said.

We all looked at her.

"I want you to take Monique back East. You'll teach her English and how to run the business. The women of Philadelphia won't know anything of her past, and she'll have a clean start in life."

Phoebe looked at Monique.

Rose said, "Trust me, they're going to adore her! She's got the look, the style, and the charisma. When you're ready to open your second location, she'll manage the first."

Phoebe looked doubtful. "I hadn't given much thought to a second location."

"Well, you should, because I've got lots of potions, and you'll need to be accessible to the masses."

Phoebe smiled. "I like the way you think," she said.

She waited for Rose to translate the idea to Monique. As she spoke, Monique's eyes grew larger. When Rose stopped speakin', Monique gave Phoebe a hopeful look, and said somethin' to her in French. Phoebe answered back, then Rose joined in. They started jabberin' faster and faster and could've been sayin' anythin', far as the rest of us knew. But in the end, they all hugged and were apparently in business together.

"I've got some news of my own," Rose said. "I'm adopting Hannah."

"Now there's a shock!" Gentry said, laughin'.

"Who could have seen *that* comin'?" Hester said, sarcastically.

Hannah spoke up for the first time since I'd known her. She said, "I expect we shall all die before reaching Springfield."

We were stunned at the comment. But Rose just laughed it off and said, "Hannah's not given to excessive optimism, which is a good thing. By always expecting the worst, she'll never be disappointed in life."

CHAPTER 57

WHEN WE GOT to Dodge, I took Emma, Mary, Hester, and Leah around to the brothels I knew, and waited for 'em to choose from those that wanted 'em. After gettin' 'em situated, we hugged goodbye, and bless their hearts, they each offered me a free poke next time I came through town. All 'cept Emma, who curiously showed me her four-fingered left and six-fingered right hands and offered me a "five finger discount."

Rose sold one of the wagons and its ox team, and stocked the other with enough provisions to get her, Phoebe, Hannah, and Monique to Springfield. The plan was for Shrug to escort 'em to Springfield, where they'd drop off Hannah and the wagon, and the women would continue on horseback to Rolla. After puttin' Phoebe and Monique on the train, Rose and Shrug would head back to Springfield, where Rose would devote herself to runnin' her ranch and raisin' Hannah.

"Who's gonna take care of Hannah when you go to Rolla?" Gentry said.

"Roberto and his wife. Don't worry, she'll be in good hands."

"And what will Shrug do?" Gentry said. "After he gets you back to Springfield."

Shrug smiled at Gentry, pleased to hear her worryin' about his future.

Rose said, "Shrug knows he's always welcome at my place. Forever, if it suits him."

"I s'pect it'll suit him," I said. "You're the best cook in the county and have a well-stocked liquor cabinet."

Shrug smiled.

Gentry looked at me.

"I guess you and me are gonna run a saloon and card emporium in Dodge City," she said.

"I guess we're gonna. If I can pay for it."

"How much will it cost?"

"A lot."

"How much you got?"

"Not much."

"So what are we gonna do?"

I smiled. "What if I told you I know where there's a trunk hid under a man's bed that might be filled with cash or gold?"

Gentry's face bloomed into a beautiful smile. "I'd like to see it!"

"Even if it turns out there's no money in it?"

"Either way, it'll be an adventure, and we'll be together."

It was, and we were.

THE END

Special Offer from John Locke!

If you like my books, you'll LOVE my mailing list! By joining, you'll receive discounts of up to 67% on future eBooks. Plus, you'll be eligible for amazing contests, drawings, and you'll receive immediate notice when my newest books become available!

Visit my website:
http://www.DonovanCreed.com

John Locke

New York Times Best Selling Author
8th Member of the Kindle Million Sales Club
(which includes James Patterson, Stieg Larsson,
George R.R. Martin and Lee Child, among others)

John Locke had 4 of the top 10 eBooks on
Amazon/Kindle at the same time, including #1 and #2!

...Had 6 of the top 20, and 8 books in the top 43
at the same time!

...Has written 19 books in three years in four separate
genres, all best-sellers!

...Has been published in numerous languages by many of the
world's most prestigious publishing houses!

Donovan Creed Series:

Lethal People

Lethal Experiment

Saving Rachel

Now & Then

Wish List

A Girl Like You

Vegas Moon

The Love You Crave

Maybe

Callie's Last Dance

Emmett Love Series:

Follow the Stone

Don't Poke the Bear

Emmett & Gentry

Goodbye, Enorma

Dani Ripper Series:

Call Me

Promise You Won't Tell?

Dr. Gideon Box Series:

Bad Doctor

Box

Other:

Kill Jill

Non-Fiction:

How I Sold 1 Million eBooks in 5 Months!

CPSIA information can be obtained
at www.ICGtesting.com
Printed in the USA
FSOW03n1002081016
25902FS